# HEMINGSTEEN

"I had a wonderful novel to write about Oak Park," Hemingway said in 1952, "but never would because I did not want to hurt living people."

CHARLES FENTON
*The Apprenticeship of Ernest Hemingway*


"The imagination of a boy is healthy; and the mature imagination of a man is healthy; but there is a space of life between, in which the soul is in a ferment, the character undecided, the way of life uncertain, the ambition thick-sighted; thence proceeds . . . all the thousand bitters which men must necessarily taste."

JOHN KEATS
Preface to *Endymion*

# HEMINGSTEEN

*Michael Murphy*

## AUTOLYCUS PRESS

**SAINT LOUIS 1977**

ACKNOWLEDGEMENT

Some of the episodes in this novel appeared originally
in *Inland* magazine. Permission to reprint these is
gratefully acknowledged.

AUTOLYCUS PRESS
P.O. Box 23929
Webster Groves, Missouri 63119

**Library of Congress Cataloging in Publication Data**

Murphy, Michael, 1930-
    Hemingsteen.

    1.  Hemingway, Ernest, 1899-1961, in fiction, drama,
poetry.  I.  Title.
PZ4.M97876He        [PS3563.U746]        813'.5'4        77-9890

To

SHELDON MIX

the admirable editor of *Inland,*
who was the first to see this work
in manuscript.

# INTRODUCTION

*The idea for this book originated with Hemingway in his statement about the Oak Park novel: that, and certain of his autobiographical stories, conveyed the direction he might have taken in the writing of the novel.*

*My intention in the writing was not to be unremittingly imitative of Hemingway's style, but rather to suggest the form and posture he might have adopted toward the events in this book. I have used necessarily some techniques and devices that are identified with his work; and there is, in these fictional renderings, as in Hemingway's, a deliberate use of symbol and allegory.*

*The meanings Hemingway intended in some of his stories easily might elude the reader because of his deceptively simple style and his subtle, artful use of symbol. In his Nobel Prize speech he said, "Things may not be immediately discernible in what a man writes . . . but eventually they are quite clear, and by these, and the degree of alchemy that he possesses, he will endure or be forgotten."*

*It is hoped that the present work—a mixture of what I know as fact and what I have invented—will prosper and endure by way of certain things that may be eventually perceived in it and because it is, in its own way, right and true.*

MICHAEL MURPHY
*June,* 1977

# HEMINGSTEEN

# ONE (1917)

Then there was the summer of the year. He lay in his bed up in his room and he decided. He looked out through the window to the trees. Deciding was the easy part. He had come back home from school and set his books aside and now he lay on the bed. He had already come to his decision but he had to think about it. He turned it over in his mind that afternoon. He thought it out again that night. The hard part had to be prepared.

That night he listened to the wind outside and thought about the part he had decided and the harder part that had to be prepared. The wind was in the trees and came in through the window and was cool against his face and chest. He had come to his decision now and he would have to tell them. He would have to stick with it and they would have to know. That was in the summer of 1917.

• • •

Before he came to his decision, and in the making of it, in the process of the thinking and rethinking, as he walked on home from school, he gathered up such fragments of the past that he remembered. He walked on west on Lake to Oak

1

Park Avenue; turning then to walk on north to Erie Street. He stopped then on the corner and looked across to where his early years were spent, the years now fragile and now vague in memory. He gathered up what he remembered, shard and fading pieces of the past, putting them in order in a way that would convey some meaning, possibly; some certain and definable response.

The memories about the house were vague, and yet it was the same as he remembered it, the same two-story structure with the Queen Anne turret and the attic making it appear another story high. It was the house grandfather Abba Hall had given them, the house in which his doctor father had delivered him. He looked at it as something of a shell from out of the past, a dim and hollow place where something had occurred, where ghostly echoes sounded on a clear cold dawn or in disturbing hours of the night. It was where his childhood began and ceased to be. The house had grown smaller as he had grown larger and he saw himself inside of it—that would have been thirteen years ago, when he was four—he saw himself up in the third-floor attic that he loved.

That was where his father kept his artifacts lined up upon the shelves against the walls: the stone axeheads, the flints, the pottery, and all the

2

specimens of once-living things in milky-white liquid in the bottles that had strange names on the labels. The bottles and the artifacts were those his mother had thrown out into the yard and burned. There had been two burnings and the one that he recalled most vividly was at the new house when Grandfather Hall had gone and, with him, with his death, there were gone a lot of other once-living unseen things that nobody ever talked about.

The new house had been one-year away from this one. After Abba's death, in May of 1905, they went to Michigan that summer and came back to live inside the rented house on Grove. The new house that his mother had designed and built with Abba's money was finished then, within the year, and that was where it all began, the whatever-it-was that took the place of his childhood and that he had lost about two years ago.

Two years ago, then, that which he had lost could never be recovered. Emotions were a part of it and his father had changed, but possibly the change had taken place in him and not in his father, or very probably in both of them. There was that possibility too, and it had to involve the no-longer shooting wild geese together and the no-longer cutting through thickets and the no-longer building of wood fires in found camps. In-

3

volved as well was the conflict of directions or the view of what he thought he was and had the right to do and where to go and what his father thought he was and thought he did so badly, or perhaps it was improperly, or even, on occasion, wickedly. Involving as it did those fine and truly gratifying things that father and son had done together, the chance to do them, or the desire, lost, it was a change that could not be reversed. So all of that was lost. All the sharing slipped away, and many were denied them by his mother, so the chances too were lost, and, with the conflicts that were like a wall between the two of them, his father and himself, the other thing was lost as well.

Both lost in Ernest's mind. He turned his thoughts back to the years that had preceded all the better times, remembering and gathering, still standing looking at the child's house that he had known, the fragments of the past all gathered in his mind like pieces of a fragile structure that might topple if he moved an inch. His vision being limited to what he could recall, he found no answer in the house remembered nor in the horse and buggy and the snows that piled up against it that he still remembered, and the snows that drifted on the prairie land beyond; his father strong, sure-footed, and protective, he remembered, and farther back to all the images his father mirrored, to Grandfather Anson and his stories of the Civil War, to Uncle Tyley and to Abba's stories, too, and all the other facts and fictions that had startled and excited him and now remained alive in all that he recalled.

All of that was right, although it failed now in giving him the answer that he wanted; yet the right that he remembered had been good and still was good, as he remembered it, walking on again along the brick-laid street. The trees were greenleafed arches overhead and sifted of the sunlight as he walked on under them and worked the past and future in his mind. He had stepped into the shadow of its presence, he had brushed against the answer and he knew that it was something truly strong and possibly exalted as the trees and distances beyond; but still the shape and form of it eluded him.

He knew that it was there; he did not know precisely what it was. Then there was the other thing —his mother somehow was a part of it, his father was a party of the second part and he was in the middle of a conflict that would find no resolution without understanding. And there was no understanding. And, lacking that, there was no resolution either.

Then the form and shape of it eluded him and then he lay upstairs and looked out to the trees that afternoon. He thought about his writing and the stories he had written for the *Tabula.* He thought about them then again that night and they were not as fine as he had thought. But that was possibly a part of what and where the form and resolution would be found. They were splendid stories at the time that they were written, now they were not so splendid, nor was hunting with his father, talking with his mother, playing with his sisters and his little brother, hiking with his friends, nor football, track, and swimming, and the boys and all the girls. Nothing, or almost nothing, that had been any good was any longer any good. Nor right and proper for the thing for which he yearned.

• • •

That morning, the morning after he had come to his decision, his sister Marcelline came into the room. She came to gather up the books that he had borrowed from the village library. Now that school was out, and now that all of them were making summer plans, she had to take their borrowed books back to the Scoville Institute: that was the village library.

"Want to come along?" she said.

ONE (1917)

"No," he said, "I got things to do."

"Like what?"

He hadn't wanted to be that way with her. She would be leaving soon for Oberlin. He would have wanted to be pleasant but he had to be alone. Anyway, he had to go on back to school to get the shoes and books and other things that he had left that he would want to keep. He had to be alone to think.

"Like what do you have to do?" she pursued.

"Nothing," he said, "but I'll think of something."

But he knew that he was going to go to Kansas City.

7

# TWO (1914)

They went into the lunchroom and sat down at the counter. They were tired from the hiking and they had terrific thirsts. Lewis Clarahan was out of breath. Proctor Gilbert sneezed and you could see the spray of spittle from his mouth against the sunlight coming through the window. Lewis asked would Ernest put his knapsack on the stool beside him. Ernest put it there and looked on down the counter as they waited. Two men were sitting at the counter eating breakfast. They were dressed in mole-skin pants and checked shirts. They could have been game wardens or the local cops.

"What about that carp?" Proctor Gilbert said.

"I can't believe it," Lew Clarahan said. "If I hadn't seen it with my own eyes . . . ."

"That's nothing," Ernest said.

"I never saw a catch like that before," Proctor Gilbert said.

"My father bagged half that much again once." He looked on down the counter at the two men eating. One of them had a triangular shaped pock-scarred face. His mouth was thin and straight, a long straight line across his face. The other one was fat. And, as he ate, his fat cheeks moved back

8

and forward like pieces of rubber stuck on to his face.

"What'll you have, boys?" the counter man said.

"Something cold, some pop," Ernest said.

"I don't know," Procter Gilbert said.

"What's yours?" the counter man looked at Clarahan.

"I'll have cream soda," he said.

"We don't have it."

"I'll take strawberry," Ernest said.

"We don't have that either," said the counter man.

"Okay, what do you have?" he said, looking down the counter at the two men eating.

"We got root beer, lime, ginger ale."

"I'll have root beer," Proctor Gilbert said.

"Okay with me," Lewis said.

Ernest thought a moment, then he looked at him and said. "Make mine ginger ale." He was tired from the hiking and he didn't really care, just as long as it was cold and wet. They had been all along the new canal through Summit. Starting early in the morning, they had hiked a distance and had seen some pheasants and a northern owl. They had tried to catch a weasel; Proctor, who almost had it, stumbled over a branch and fell right down in the water of the canal.

9

"You still wet, Proc?" Ernest looked beyond Clarahan at Gilbert. Gilbert was putting sugar in the cupped palm of his hand and licking it up.

"Yeah, a little," Proctor said. "I should have taken off the belt, it's still wet."

"You get a canvas belt like that wet," Ernest said, "and it might just shrink up and strangle you."

Lew and Proctor Gilbert laughed and Ernest looked back down the counter at the two men eating. He was thinking of that time that Clarahan and he and Savage all went skinny-dipping in the Des Plaines River. Superintendent Fogg of the Academy came walking by and saw them. Savage went running up the bank with his big privates shaking and he went screaming like an Indian and then fell down laughing, he didn't give a damn. But Lew had been a little scared and they had to tell him that it didn't mean nothing, old Fogg couldn't do nothing about it anyway.

The counter man went over to the two men eating and asked was there anything else.

"Coffee," the fat one said. His voice was low and rasping.

"Coffee," said the other one. He pushed his plate forward and put his elbows on the counter.

"What kind of a place is it," the fat one said to

the one with his elbows on the counter, "where they don't give you no God damn coffee with your eats?"

"A joint like this," the other one said. His lips hardly moved when he talked, they were just a straight thin line across his face.

"A God damn slop joint," the fat one said.

Then the counter man brought their coffee. His hands were shaking and the cups began to rattle in the saucers as he set them down. "Will that be all, gentlemen?" he said.

The fat one looked up at him and over at the thin one. He said out of the corner of his mouth, "He called you a gentleman, Jack."

"Well, ain't that pretty," Jack said. He slurped his coffee through his tight straight mouth with a noise you could have heard a block away. "That makes three of us, I guess."

And when they got up to pay, the fat one took his cup of coffee, what was left inside the cup, and splashed it all out over the counter. "Your coffee is slop," he said.

They left some money and went out the door, the one called Jack holding back the screen door, looking in. "Slop," he said back at the counter man and banged the screen door shut.

The counter man picked up the money they

had left and looked over at the door. He took a long deep breath and shook his head and walked slowly on down the counter.

"What was eating *them?*" Ernest asked.

"I don't know," he said. "I figure they was mad from that poker game over at Stackpole's last night. I heard there was some big stakes lost."

"What were they, gamblers or something?"

The counter man was counting out the money and he said, not looking at him, "No, they been working on the canal with the Federal Engineers. Those guys go out when there's a payday and they blow their pay in a game and they take it out on somebody else."

"It ain't right," Ernest said.

"Well, they're big tippers," the counter man said, putting all the money in a drawer.

"Yeah, what'd they leave you?" Clarahan wanted to know.

"Nothing," said the counter man.

"A couple of cruts, that's what they are," Ernest said.

"Well, we can't leave you no tip neither," Proctor Gilbert said.

"That's okay, boys, I got plenty comes in here and gives me big tips all the time. It's the ones that mess up like those two that never leave no tip.

You can always tell 'em. You can see 'em coming from a mile off."

Ernest handed Clarahan his knapsack and he wiped the counter off with his shirt sleeve and left it clean and shining where the sweat mark from his palm had been. They went on out then and they closed the door very carefully and went on down the road and through the town of Summit and began the long hike back along the new canal.

# THREE (1914)

Ernest threw a wild right at him. If it had landed it would have killed the little crut. Then Phil came back at him with two sharp, lightning-fast jabs that caught him by surprise.

Ernest backed off. "Hey, you hit below the belt, you crut."

"That's a damn lie," Phil White said.

They were in the alley back of the church. The fight had been coming on now for a long time and it had to happen. They feinted, dancing back and forward, right and left, jabbing at the air. They danced in circles, feinting now and again. The alley dust began to cloud up around their feet. Overhead, the sky was darkening and rain began to fall, you could hear it pinging against the slate roof of the church; it left tiny perforations in the fine dirt in the alley.

The fight that had been coming on now for a long time went back to names and threats. It came out of rivalries that started on the swimming teams and on the three-miler River Forest run. It started anyway with vicious names and insults and with threats. It was ending now behind the church on their agreement that what might happen would be kept a secret with the two of them and neither one would talk about the outcome.

But White had really hit him below the belt. Ernest came back at him with both arms flailing and he struck a solid rib-cracking blow against White's chest. Phil started feinting with his left and then began to lead and scored a left-hand hook against the jaw. Ernest tried to push him off. Phil cut loose then with his right and sidestepped Ernest's left and moved on in with one fast, two fast, three fast fist-hard jolts against the temple.

Ernest felt it sting. He backed off quickly. He felt an aching numbness at his temple and he stood back, almost crying, and he said, "Whataya trying to do, Phil? You can kill a guy hitting on the temples like that. Christ, don't you know that? You can *kill* a guy that way."

"You asked for it," White said. "You've been asking for it for a long time, Steen." He held his fists tight hard and ready. They were reddened at the knuckles and his face was flushed up too.

"That don't give you no right to try and kill me. That's a hell of a thing to do, White."

"Look, you asked for it. You got no right to call me names the way you did. You asked for it plenty of times."

Ernest jumped him then. He was mad enough

to kill him and he moved straight on in with one quick jab and then cut loose a fast hard right that whacked against White's jaw and knocked him back so he could hardly keep his balance and he stumbled backwards on his heels in the dirt and almost fell.

But White got back to face him and he went into a forward crouch and glared at him with hatred in his eyes. And then he cried out, "Bastard," and he came at him and pivoted and took him unawares. Ernest was afraid. He was powerless to get his arms up to his head to block the rain of blows of White's assault.

White was mad and had the reach on him. You could see it in his eyes, he wasn't going to lose this one. He struck him on the nose and eyes and jaw with half a dozen jabs that Ernest couldn't block or counter.

Ernest tasted blood. He heard the crunching of Phil White's knuckles on his jaw and felt the quick sharp blows that felt quite dull and deadened at the start and then began to hurt like hell. First it was his nose, he thought his God damn nose was broken. White had fouled him, he had whacked his wrist across his nose. Then it was the spreading pain around his eyes and cheekbones and his God damn face was burning like it had been

16

torched and beaten to a pulp. He was finished and he knew it.

He had to let White know that he was finished. He knew that White had beaten him and he had to let him know. It was a hell of a thing to have to admit that this pint-sized punk had beaten him. That was the hell of it but even that was not the worst. He wasn't going to shake his hand, he wasn't going to give him that satisfaction. But God-dammit why did he have to let him see him cry? That was the shame of it, the worst of it, to let him see you cry. You could have your head beat in and you would get it back. But not the shame of it, not the shame of crying, you could not forget that ever. Bawling like that was just about the worst shameful thing that you could ever do.

"It's okay, Steen, what the hell."

Ernest kept his back to him. He wasn't going to answer. His nose was bleeding. His God damn nose was broken.

"Look, Steen, what the hell."

Christ what was he ever going to say to anybody after this?

"Look, I just caught you a little off guard. Forget it. Steen."

Ernest walked away from him, slowly going on down the alley to the corner of the church. The

17

rain had let up but the sky was dark. He looked at the garbage cans. He kicked a piece of cardboard in his path and walked on holding his arm up to his face to keep the blood from dripping from his bleeding nose.

"Hey, Steen," White called after him. "What the hell."

Ernest went on slowly and on around the corner of the church. He didn't want to have to talk to anybody and he didn't want to talk to White, least of all to White. He wished the rain would come.

"Steen."

They were not going to be any kind of friends again.

"Steen."

He wasn't going to be even talking to White again.

•  •  •

It was six months later that he talked to White. That was after he had made his trip to Walker's Gym. He told him that he was well aware that he had beaten him, that he, White, was better at the time. But now he knew a few things himself that he hadn't know about the boxing trade and if White was ever going to talk too much about the incident behind the church then he was going to beat him to a pulp.

• • •

What the hell. He went on slowly on around the corner of the church and crossed the street and went across the park. White was going to pay for it, he would see to that. He was going to kill the bastard with his shotgun. Now the rain began to come down in a shower. He felt better with the rain now beating down on him and watched the blood mix with the rain and thin out on the back of his hand. He was going on down to Walker's Gym and he was going to get him. He was going to learn all that a guy could learn at Walker's Gym. He was going to get Phil White.

• • •

Walker's Gym had this policy nobody ever told you about if you were a fresh punk kid who thought you were Stan Ketchell or Fitzsimmons. Nobody ever told you about it because it was one of their private little jokes that gave the boys some jollying when no new cards were shaping up.

The policy they had then that nobody ever told you about was still around that Saturday when Ernest walked in thinking he was going to walk out having all the moxey that had been passed on down from Dan Mendoza to Fitzsimmons that would guarantee that no Phil White or Pentecost or any other big or little threat the other side of

Austin Avenue was ever going to blowhard around that he had bested or had busted Ernest Hemingway.

So then he saw the ring where big-gloved boxers in oversize black trunks and flannel shirts were sparring off against the ropes. It smelled like somebody had left a bag of rotten fruit around. Along the wall he saw a group of photographs in dull black frames and looked them over closely, picking up the names that he had heard or read about. He looked at all the pictures and he turned to look back at the ring when the sparring boxers made the grunts and groans that sounded like stricken animals far off somewhere in a clearing.

One of the photographs was signed by Big Jim Jeffries himself, dated 1899, and Ernest read, "This mug is a good friend to George Siler who did the counting." Siler, he learned later, was the ref when Jeffries took the crown from Fitzsimmons at old Coney Island. He learned that Siler was a trainer there at Walker's and he met him sometime after and he learned a lot from him.

There were old dulled prints of Corbett too and old John L. himself in knee-length belted tights and small white gloves, and then on down the wall a picture of Bob Fitzsimmons in a pose that showed his big back muscles rippling and his head

gone almost bald. Under it, stuck in the corner of
the frame, someone had written on a piece of yel-
lowed paper, "Fitz when he was here—the Greatest of Them All."

Another one of Jeffries dated 1910 with someone named Mike Murphy in the corner of the ring
and under it the caption, "Mike posed with Big
Jim day before the 'Long Melford.'" Murphy,
Ernest later learned, was the trainer who had said
that Jeffries, who was 35, had too much fat around
the kidneys ever to defeat Jack Johnson. The
"Long Melford" was the straight left in the 15th
round that ended Big Jim's great career.

He spent a lot of time just looking at the prints
of all the greats along the wall and reading tacked-
up pages of Frank Leslie's *Illustrated Weekly,* dated
1892. But he felt nervous standing there and looking and he walked on to the end, off to the corner
of the room. There was a punching bag he pushed
at slightly with his fist, he did not take a real swing
at it because he did not want to be conspicuous.

He saw a boxer in long shorts who was running
standing-still and then he saw the man who came
out of the door marked Manager who went up to
the boxer, talking to him as the boxer feinted,
shadow-boxing, in a circle motion next to him.
The boxer rolled his head and feinted.

The other man was goateed and well-dressed. His hair and beard were grayish-white. He wore a light gray suit and purple vest. The watch chain on the vest was gold and had a bright gilt medal hanging from it. His coat was British, long and big-lapelled and cutaway in back. Ernest overheard him call the other "Busch." "Watch your distance, Busch. Keep it 13 inches." He pointed down to the fighter's feet. "There. And keep your right foot at an angle. Forty-five degrees. The toe, like this."

And the goateed man positioned himself to illustrate. His shoes were patent-leather, or as shiny as, and he wore gray spats that looked like moleskin that, in colour, matched his coat.

"Why's the weight on the left, Colonel?" Busch was asking. He was sweating. He kept moving all the time. He had terrific muscles on his back and thighs and when he moved they rippled and were shiny with sweat.

"Because," the Colonel said, "you have to consider the center of gravity of your body. Now keep your left leg straight, or nearly straight. No, no, not stiff."

"That's right," Busch said, moving in the circle, and he kept his left leg straight.

The other man called the Colonel looked over

then at Ernest. Ernest turned back to one of the pictures on the wall. The Colonel said, talking to Busch, "I saw you with 'The Dancer.' You made a bad mistake. You have to learn that you must quarter-face your adversary. Don't give him a full-faced target, boy. Be rational about it."

Busch looked at the Colonel. He had stopped dancing around now and he was looking at the Colonel with a dumb dog-like look.

"Rational, Busch. I assume you are unaware of the meaning of the word rational?"

Busch nodded. He was like a dog the way he looked.

"Never mind," the Colonel said. "See what that young man wants."

•  •  •

And that was how it all began, with Busch asking him what was it. It was like a nightmare after that. Ernest remained at Walker's Gym two hours. And when he left, he had a cut below his right eye. He had a broken rib, or what seemed broken when he felt of it. His nose was stuffed up with clotted blood. His shirt was bloodied dark red all down the front. And all across his back, around the beltline, where Busch had rabbit-punched him, he felt a soreness and a painful aching that went down to his buttocks to his legs. He also knew what resin on the boards was like: Busch had knocked him down a couple times. Busch laughed. He knocked you down and then he always laughed. And all that he had done was ask if somebody there could teach you how to box.

That was when they called their little meeting, with the Colonel and a couple plug-uglies who trained and worked as seconds for such fighters as McCoy and Smith and Brennen, and who were themselves old scrappers who had lost their chances, one of them badsighted and the other one all crippled in one leg. Both had broken noses; one had cauliflower ears. So they were in on it and Busch had won the toss or whatever way they had decided with. And all that he had done was ask if someone there could teach him how to box.

And sure they had a teacher there in Busch, who was a God damn killer, only they didn't get around to telling you and you had to learn the hardest way, so they put you in the ring with him, and it was like you had gone and killed his mother or something worse, and Busch was out to teach you plenty, mainly not to fight with anyone who was a mucking sadist and who laughed whenever you were clouted hard or down. And all that he

24

had done was ask if somebody there would teach him how to box.

It was a week before it stopped, the ringing in his ears. And then the Colonel's words, oh he was never going to forget the Colonel's words. It was like a nightmare, that lecture from the Colonel when Busch had finished him and went off laughing to the dressing room. He was standing there and bleeding and about to cry and all the Colonel said was, "There are no two pugilists whose position is precisely alike. The arm is the principal motive power physically given to man for offense and defense. A man without a brain cannot become a boxer . . ."

It was like a nightmare.

Ernest stepped outside into the air. He felt like he had stepped from hell into another world. The Colonel's phrases churned around like snakes inside his head, and with the ringing in his ears, and he was shaking terribly. He knew absolutely that he was going to be sick. He kept hearing Busch's words—"You got enough, kid?" He was shaking plenty.

All that crap the Colonel told him with him standing there bleeding all over the God damn floor. "Pugnacious pugilism," the Colonel said. Crap. What the hell did he think he was, God Almighty?

All he had done was ask.

· · ·

So they had this policy that if you come around and ask they beat the stuffing out of you. And guys like Busch and all the other plug-uglies lapped it up. It was one big laugh for all of them all right. Well, nobody, or almost nobody, who ever asked and got his guts beat out of him, nobody ever came back.

One of them did, though: Gunboat Sweeney was what they called him, and he was Lightweight Champion of the World.

· · ·

On the Saturday following his first and most important lesson in the manly art, at exactly nine o'clock, Ernest Hemingway went back to Walker's Gym.

The Colonel was the first to encounter him.

The Colonel looked at him for a long time, then he pulled his big pocket watch out on the chain with the boxing medal on it and he looked down at the watch and then he put it back in the pocket of his purple vest. "Nine o'clock," he said.

Ernest looked at him and grinned. His upper lip was swollen so that smiling was still a little painful.

"Very well then, boy," the Colonel said. "I'm going to make a boxer out of you."

26

He took him by the arm and took him to his office. He turned and looked at him. "Well, what should we call today?" he said.

Ernest had no answer.

"Well, why don't we simply call it 'Lesson Number One'?" the Colonel said.

# FOUR (1911)

"Because he is a menace," Ernest's father said.

"A menace?"

"He is not only mean but sneaky. Yes, he is one of the crookedest birds there is."

"Let's shoot them all," he said.

"Now, you may not want to do that, son. I don't mean the crow is not a noble bird. He is so cunning that we must grant him the right to life as one of the noblest birds of all."

"But you said he was crooked."

"Quite so. But it is only if we put our wits and cunning against his wits and cunning that we are being sportsmanlike. It's possible to shoot them, well enough. I know one shooter who brought down a thousand in a single year."

"A whole thousand?"

"He made a study of it. He took the time to do it right, to outwit the bird."

"How did he do that?"

"He lured them with large stuffed owls."

"They eat owls?"

"He fastened the owls to the tops of poles in open spaces. He could hoot like one. Like this," and his father hooted and he sounded like an owl, all right. Ernest was amazed. He would try it out on his own and bring the crows in. He would learn the way to bring them in and shoot them. He would shoot them and would bring the dead ones to his father and would tell him he had done it fairly with the owls and everything.

They were walking in the fields west of the Des Plaines River, west of the pines and birches, out where the prairie land spread wide and off into the russet-coloured bunches on the rolling hummocks far ahead, across the woodchuck holes and muskrat mounds along the shallow water ponds, into the grainless growthless fields, then across the hummocks to the trees where there were birds on branches, where the crows were waiting to outwit them with their cunning and their faint because distant "caw-caws."

"I can hear one," Ernest said.

"Must have heard my owl. Let me try a call."

And then his father stopped and did a crow call and they got an answer and he said, "They're up ahead. We'll have some crows to shoot, if I'm not mistaken."

His father was never mistaken. They kept on walking.

"You have to learn distress calls," his father said.

"Like what?"

29

"The young crows. That will bring the old ones out. I'll show you how to do it later. We'll have to have some paper."

"But you did it already and he answered."

His father laughed. They kept on walking toward the hummocks and the trees, his father laughed and said, "He's much too smart to fall for that. He might answer but he won't show himself. Not yet."

"If you do the owl, would owls come out?"

"No, not the owls." He did an owl again, "Whoo wh-hoo, wh-o-o wh-o-o." Again the crow made answer. "See, it works."

"Gee, that was good. Do you think we can get him?"

"If we can get up there in that clump of bushes and call him with a teasing or a fighting strain. We may have timed it wrong for any there might be back there."

"Where?"

"Where they are. I know they're back there. In the trees. They may be feeding back there, you can't tell. They can feed at any time, of course, and nearly anything will do. They like the eggs of wild game-birds. They attack the nest, you see. They sometimes feed quite late, before the sun goes down, and that's the best time to go a-gunning for them. They mop up on the farmer's fields after seeding time. And if you know where nests are, you'll find them. And when the wild game is scarce, they'll pack up for a barnyard."

"Why is that?"

"Well, any farmer can answer that for you. The crow will eat the chicken eggs, you see. That's a favorite. There's almost nothing that he won't go to. But that's where cunning is the proper way to get them. Even though they're crooked, you have to be quite fair in shooting them. I prefer to lure them with a call, or use an owl, the way the fellow did I told you of. Except I wouldn't go shooting for a thousand of them. That's not real sport, you see. You can hunt them any time and everywhere, but not to be unsportsmanlike."

"What's the best gun, Father?"

"Well, that's all about the same, a 12- or 20-gauge, it's all the same, and any shot, any size you have. For powder, though, I prefer Ballistite. You can use your odds-and-ends on crows. Push the shot off properly, and, if your range is right, that's all you need. But you can be a sport about it. Old blackfeathers has a chance to get away."

"Not with you he don't."

His father looked down at him. His eyes were bright and wrinkled when he smiled. His father

31

liked to talk and liked to tell his son all that he knew. And he knew everything.

•   •   •

Once he asked his father though if crows were the most cunning and dangerous critters around and his father said no, no they were not.

"People are," he said. "You'll have to learn that, son. It's something I can't teach you. But you'll learn it all the same. They will teach you in the worst way possible. Unsportsmanlike. But you will learn about the meanness and the cunning of your fellow man in time."

# FIVE (1915)

"He was a man of talent and a fine mannered person. A person of refinement. He achieved great eminence as a professor of music."

"Yes, Mother."

It was Sequence Number Seven in the long and neverending recitation of his maternal ancestry. The urge had come upon his mother again on that Sunday afternoon; the opportunity too, and she had captured him just as his father went out to deliver the new Sutphen baby. It was the new baby happening that got her started. She had him at the table in the dining room. He could look out the window and see the shed and trees out back. That was all. He could see her too and sometimes, because of her, he could not see clearly out the window. She had him pinned against the wall.

"That's why it's ever so important for you to practice your cello," she was saying.

"Yes, Mother."

"Not only is the instrument itself a thing of beauty, but you come to your musical talent quite naturally, don't you see?"

"Yes, Mother."

"We have the tradition, the musical talent that

33

began, as far as we know, in the early 18th Century. And then it may have even gone back to Malcolm, we don't know."

"That was the King of Scotland," he said.

"Yes. And the Earl of Warwick too, of course."

Oh yes, the Earl of Warwick, the "kingmaker."

"He was called the 'Kingmaker,'" she said.

"Yes, I know," he said.

"But it was Edward Miller who revolutionized the Church of England music. Before his time, they had used the services of a leader to line out a phrase at a time, to be repeated by the worshippers, without hymn-books or accompaniment."

Ernest did not want to ask her any questions that would prolong it. She would be getting back to Miller soon, that being the name she had given him to fit between his other two. It was the one he changed so often in his bylines for the paper, to Monahan, Macnamara, and even Michaelowitch. He had wanted to change Ernest too, and even Hemingway, and had, a couple times: He favored Ring, after Lardner, and Stein and Hemingway-stein, after their pawn-shop joke, the "Three Ball Joint" of Cohen, that was Ohlsen, Goldberg, that was Golder, and himself. Pomeroy it was who started "Steen." Stein and Steen and Hemingstein, the pronunciations changed.

34

"He also wrote the 'History of Doncaster,'" his mother said, "so that you know where you came by your interest in writing."

"Yes, Mother." And he had always thought his interest in writing was from Miss Dixon and Fannie Biggs and himself. He never knew Edward Miller had started it all more than one hundred years ago.

"William was trained to his music. Now it may be that you will succeed in becoming a writer, and a good one, but you have to take into account that good trained musicians are always needed, and it's an altogether respectable line of endeavor, a professional line."

"Yes, Mother."

He wanted to tell her that he had no talent for the cello and that the musical genius in the family had achieved perfection with her. She should have accepted that offer from the Met. Perhaps he would tell her that to flatter her. But that would only serve then to prolong it. She had taken a chair and he knew that she was going to go on.

"About this time, some of his gay and reckless companions dared him to fiddle his way to the court of 'Tippoo Saib,' the reigning Prince of India. He took the dare. He had only his violin, you understand, and yet he took ship. Well, his father rushed to the dock and tossed him a packet of letters of introduction to prominent people in India. Do you know what the young scamp did?"

Jumped overboard? "No, Mother, what did he do?"

"He tossed the letters overboard, right in sight of his father."

Ernest tried to force a laugh but it wasn't much. He always liked the part about India even though he wasn't sure of the truth of it. And yet his mother always stuck with the story, she had it all down in her mind the way he was hearing it now, and it was the same as she had told it before. He hoped she was going to skip some parts between India and the hard times of 1857. He loved to hear about his grandfather's hard times when the banks failed and the business houses closed. He liked to hear about Mr. Trick especially. Mr. Trick was the General Store manager. The name Bill Trick, he thought, was the neatest name he had ever heard.

"He spent six years at the court of Tippoo Saib, making money with his splendid organ performances as well as his violin."

Ernest had a vision of young William trying to get aboard ship with his organ.

"There are at least four stories of how he

was presented with a priceless Cremona by the Prince. . . ."

Ernest looked out the window beyond her shoulder and watched the windblown branches of the tree while she went on about the court in India. He wished that priceless Cremona were still around. She was still talking about it when his father got back.

•  •  •

Dr. Clarence Hemingway was flushed and breathless. He rushed into the dining room without even taking off his hat and announced that he had just delivered another Sutphen. "A good one this time, nine pounds if he's an ounce."

"Clarence," Ernest's mother said.

"I'll never know how Jack's going to feed that brood of his," he said. "Nowadays, it's a constant struggle, just making ends meet."

"Clarence, haven't you forgotten something, dear?" she said.

He removed his hat. "I plumb forgot," he said.

He turned to put it on the corner table. "Well, boy," he said, turning back to Ernest, and looking fine and vigorous, and happy too, "what say we take a spin out to the mounds?"

Ernest got up. That was better news than he had hoped for.

"Clarence," she said. "I thought that Ernest might put in a little practice."

"Mother, it's Sunday," Ernest said. "I never practice on Sunday."

"That's right," his father said.

"I don't recall that you practiced Friday night."

"Golly, Mother, that was Friday night. We had track and field trials."

"I'm not sure that track and field are more important than your practice."

"Well maybe it isn't, Mother. But that's part of school. That's something I got to do. They count on me."

"So does your talent count on you, young man. If you don't practice, your talent is wasted, and that's quite wrong. Don't you agree?"

"Yes, Mother. But the Good Lord said that Sunday was a day of rest. He didn't say anything about practicing your cello on Sunday."

"Don't become sacrilegious now, young man." She sat in the chair and looked up at him with stern locked eyes. But looked then at his father too and then he saw the faint suggestion of a smile on her lips. "Perhaps you're right about Sunday, Ernest. Don't you believe he's right, dear?"

"Frankly, Gracie, I think he is," his father said.

"But then," she said, "the Good Lord said nothing about hunting on Sunday that I can recollect."

"That's right," his father said quickly. "That's why we're going on a historic exploration of the Indian mounds. No hunting, just digging. An education for the boy, Gracie."

She looked at her husband and she thought a moment. She looked at him quite carefully. "Well, I suppose," she said at last.

"Then if he ever finds himself with a responsibility like Jack Sutphen, he'll be better equipped to take care of it."

"How's Martha doing?" she said.

"Fine, just fine. She's a remarkable woman, I'll have to say that."

"And Jack Sutphen's a remarkable man," she said, getting up from the chair. "He remains at home with his family on Sundays," she said as she left the room.

His father looked at him and then he followed her into the living room. "Gracie," his father said, "I promise that we'll stay home next Sunday."

• • •

Outside, his father put his arm around him. He moved close to Ernest's ear and said, "Sure Jack stays home on Sundays. That's why they have so many kids."

Ernest wanted to laugh but he did not laugh. He wanted to enjoy hearing his father laughing for a change.

# SIX (1 9 1 5)

That November afternoon in the Oxford Room Ernest read his story to the other members of the class. He stood by the big fireplace under the fretted beam ceiling. The midafternoon light of the autumn sky filtered through the stained-glass windows of the room and fell in jagged and angular patterns on the tile floor and on the rows of highbacked oaken chairs.

He stood with the pale yellow light that filtered through the northside leaded stained-glass window falling on his wetted-down combed black hair and he read his story to the English class. On both sides of him on the red brick of the fireplace with the big fire cradle were embossed quotations, one from the Greek and the other from Chaucer. The Greek "Ta Garist" was the motto of the school and it meant "the best."

His story was the best in the class of the term to date and he stood between the quotations and the brass sconces and he faced the huge oaken bench and the rows of high-backed oaken chairs the students sat in. Miss Dixon introduced him with a remark about the history of the Oxford Room.

"John Calvin Hanna," she said, the first super-

41

intendent of Oak Park and River Forest Township High School, "had planned this room, and the Greek Room, in order to identify and preserve the respective traditions they represent, not only in form and architecture, but also in the ideals of the cultures and the civilizations for which they stand."

Miss Dixon went on to point out that the Chaucer quotation—"And gladly wolde he learne and gladly teache"—was a charge that all of them must take to heart, "for whether you think of yourselves as teachers or not," she said, "you shall be teachers throughout your lives. You will teach your own children and your children's children. You will teach your neighbors and your friends. I need say nothing further about that, and I am sure that you are all anxious to hear the story Ernest Hemingway has written. It is a story from which we can all learn something, so that Ernest too, today in truth and reality, will be our teacher. He has, as Chaucer said, gladly learned, and now he teaches gladly. Ernest, you may now read your story for the class."

"Thank you, Miss Dixon," and from the beginning his voice was strained and self-consciously high-pitched. He read his story and he looked up once or twice to face the forbidding, inspecting eyes of the students seated in the high-backed oaken chairs. After that, he glanced up only at the back wall of the room and down at the large oaken bench in front of him. He wanted to keep his mind on the story as he read but he was thinking of his matted hair that he sensed was falling from the wet-combed fullness on the right side of his head and thinking too that the pages in his hands were shaking. He stood with an awkward leaning on the right foot, then the left, and then he stumbled over his own words too. He began to stammer stupidly. Wrong, he thought, and then read consciously in elevated harsher tones that made him feel foolish in the end and made him, as he finished, more embarrassed as the class applauded with restraint. He looked out at them and some had looks of self-satisfied mockery, they were happy about the way it had gone.

• • •

On his way home he felt forlorn and as an outcast and he thought, Boy, are you stupid, you are the biggest stupid jack in the whole damn school.

After that, he did not care for public readings. He had read the best story written in the class and he had read the worst reading ever and now he hated himself for being nervous and stupid. He would never go back to the Oxford Room without thinking back on his defeat. But he would go back and he would read again but he would never face a public group again without remembering that afternoon. He would avoid it if he could. He would have to do it but he would avoid it whenever that was possible.

He typed up a self-effacing, tongue-in-cheek review of his reading for the *Trapeze* but it was just an exercise, it did not belong, and it did not appear. It did not belong. And neither did he.

•   •   •

But at the dinner table in the family dining room that night he had recovered and he told his parents all about his triumph in the Oxford Room that afternoon. "The class got up on their feet and applauded," he said.

"Well, perhaps you have the makings of a good public orator," his father said.

"I think I would rather just write," he said, looking down at his hands on the table.

"Please pass the salt," his mother said.

Salting her food she said, "All expressive endeavors are good for a person in his social postures. They give one a sense of confidence. In my talks before the Oak Park Art League, I've adapted to an extemporaneous manner of speaking.

One can develop a facility, and one can gain in expressive—" she stopped and cleared her throat. "Ernest, are you listening?"

"Yes, Mother."

She went on. She went on and on and he was sorry then that he had ever brought the subject up.

## SEVEN (1915)

A bad dream woke him early. He lay in bed for a while. He could not go back to sleep. He got up then and dressed and went down stairs. His father was in the kitchen, boiling water at the stove.

He said hello, sleepily, and his father, always cheerful in the morning, said, "Good morning. What are you doing up at this unholy hour?"

He answered that he couldn't sleep. He sat down at the table. His father was preparing some coffee. Ernest stared fixedly at the blue flames of the gas on the stove. His father seemed to be in a very good mood.

"The coffee smells good," Ernest said.

"I'll pour you a cup," his father said, turning to look at him.

His father made coffee in different ways. Out camping, he simply poured the water right in with the grounds and let the grounds settle, pouring the coffee out very carefully; now he boiled it in one pot and used a sieve. He had talked of "sheep-herder's coffee" once, "when you don't bother to take the old grounds out, just put the new right on top. It's the lazy way of doing it. It's strong, you can be sure of that."

Ernest watched his father at the stove warming

46

his hands over the flames, rubbing the palms together and then each palm over the back of the other hand.

"It would be a swell day for the woods," Ernest said.

"Yes, it would."

His father looked different at this time of the morning. His face was puffy and his eyes were narrowed. His beard was scruffy and his hair uncombed. But he was always cheerful in the morning. Ernest remembered all the times they'd made camp, how cheerful his father was.

"So, you'd like to sample Dr. Hemingway's special brew?"

"Fine. I'd like to try it."

His father poured him a cup very slowly, trying not to stir up the grounds. It smelled very good.

He sat down across from him at the table. The burners were still on, warming the kitchen.

His father looked down at his coffee and Ernest remained transfixed by the blue flames of the gas. "I guess you'll have some snow to shovel today," his father said.

"Yes, sir."

"School work done?"

"I did it yesterday."

"Any problems?"

"No, sir, it's fine. I'm going out for football."

"Good." He said nothing for awhile, then he put down his cup and said, "How's the coffee?"

"Good. Very good."

His father cleared his throat and said, "Well, I'll try to get out to all the games this year."

"I hope you can."

His father made a slurping sound drinking from the cup. "How about college? Given any thought to it?"

"No, sir, not yet."

"Well, there's plenty of time. All the same, I can always talk to some people if you go to Rush."

"I haven't thought much about it yet."

"Well, no hurry, of course. There's still suffi-cient time. It's changing now, of course. Far more crowded."

"Yes, sir, I know it is."

"Well, I'll be seeing some of my friends from Rush today. Sharp and Smith's unveiling my new forceps for the College of Surgeons."

His father had first designed his laminectomy forceps before he married. That was the first, crude design, sketched out when he was sitting with Grace Hall on the banks of the Des Plaines River. Sharp and Smith had made a model of the forceps, and his father had then improved upon it, and now he was presenting it to the surgeons.

48

"Gee, that's great," Ernest said.

"Well, it's not a big affair or anything. Just a few of my friends from Rush. We'll be having a dinner, that's all."

"Are you going to make a lot of money?"

His father looked at him and smiled vaguely. "I could, if I wanted to patent the design, but that's not the point. Anything like this should not involve money."

"Don't other doctors who invent instruments make money from them?"

"Yes, some of them do, of course. But there are plenty of others who simply give over their inventions to benefit everyone, you see."

Ernest thought a moment as he sipped his coffee, then he said, "But a lot of those doctors make more money than you do."

"Certainly. Some of them do."

"You have a lot of patients you never even charge."

His father looked at him gravely and said, "Some people can't pay for services they need. Why, I can recall taking chickens from Dyer for delivering his son. The boy's about your age now. I had to deliver the boy, whether or not Dyer could pay, and the chickens were perfectly all right. We ate them, anyway."

He laughed then, thinking, and he said, "I took

49

a pig once, in the early years. That was before you were born. Old man Rufkin it was. His wife had dropsy and I had to go out every week, regular. Well, Rufkin kept a strict tabulation on my visits and then one day he says to me I ought to take the pig. Well, I didn't know, but he had already made up his mind that that was what he owed me, and so we had to tie the critter down in the buggy and I carted him right over to Slattery's for slaughter. We ate pretty good off that pig of Rufkins', and I felt I had been paid. Of course, folks never really overestimated the value of your services. They didn't know how difficult it was getting back and forth in the snow. With the horse and buggy, it was plenty hard at times."

His father was smiling and laughing and his face took on some life, some colour. He poured Ernest and himself another cup of coffee. "Getting too warm for you in here?" he said, standing at the stove.

"No, it's just about right. I'll turn the gas off later. Aren't you going to eat?"

"Well, I was going to, but I figure I'll be having lunch with some of the doctors from Rush. How about you?"

"No, thanks, I'll wait for mother."

"I can fix you some eggs."

"No, thanks anyway, Dad." He brought the cup of hot coffee to his lips and looked across at his father. "Does mother know about the forceps?"

"Oh, yes, she knows. We talked of this a long time ago. She goes along with my decision. It's all on the side of the Lord, she says, and we agree." He was thoughtful for a moment, then he said, "One has to recognize that you only have that which you give away."

Ernest looked at him. He thought a moment, then he said, "What does that mean?"

"Well, what it says. It has something to do with the feeling you get. The feeling is more important than the thing itself. I would guess it's Biblical. Your mother would know."

"But how can you give something away and still have it?"

"Well, you can. Perhaps you have to do it and then you understand. It's like somebody else said, that anything you can buy in this world isn't worth having."

Ernest pondered that; finally he said, "Well, you have to buy guns and houses and football gear, stuff like that."

"Yes," his father said, drinking his second cup of coffee, "they all have their value. But what the man said, son, is that you can't pay for the really essential things in life. You can't buy the air, the sunlight that warms you and gives us light, the trees and the waters and other things in nature. Friendship and love, you can't buy that."

"Well, sure. That's right. But take hunting—you have to buy guns to hunt."

"Do you?" he said, looking at him.

"Well, sure."

"Do you think the Indians would go along with that?"

Ernest thought about it.

His father got up from his chair and put his cup on the cutting board by the sink. "I'd best be going. I've got to catch the first 'L' for Chicago."

Ernest got up. He put his cup alongside his father's. "Well, look, Dad, I hope you have a good time. It's really swell, what you're doing."

His father, standing next to him, put his arm around his shoulder and said, "Well, that's how it works."

Dr. Hemingway went upstairs to get ready. Ernest stared at the blue flames of the gas jets burning on the stove. The colours were transparent blue, with flickers of yellow and white. There was something very mysterious and captivating about the flames. He stared at them for quite a long time before turning them off.

# EIGHT (1 9 1 5)

He had ended his sophomore year at Oak Park High and was going off for a short visit with his Uncle Tyler in Kansas City. His father had called him "son," a word he did not often use, and they were together throughout the day. They had breakfast and they went down to the basement then to see if they could find the small calfskin bag that Ernest would be taking with him.

"Maybe it's in the attic with grandfather's stuff."

"Well, it isn't here and you might be right. It could be in the old trunk up there."

"I want to find that old telescope, anyway." He meant the small field-monocular that his Grandfather Anson had used in battle during the Civil War.

Then they found the monocular up in the attic, it was stuffed behind the cushion in one corner of the wing-backed chair on which the gold brocaded cloth was stained up at the top where his grandfather had often rested his head. The chair was oak, ornately carved, it had a regal look, or aristocratic, but yet it was sturdy and solid and with much character. The carved oak arms were worn along the curled carved ends where Grandfather's hands had rubbed them smooth. Below the cushion, at the front, the fine brocaded cloth was torn through with the horsehair stuffing pushing out.

"That sure makes me think of him," Ernest said.

"Yes, I understand," his father said.

"It isn't true, is it, Father, that Grandfather was a deserter from the war?"

His father looked at him. Ernest could not see his face because of the way of the light but he knew that he was looking at him. The daylight that came through the small front window was at his father's back so that you could not see his eyes or his expression. Hairs on the edges of his sideburns and his beard stood out against the light and made his father's head look menacing. His father said, "What was that?"

"I never believed it," Ernest said.

His father was silent. He was looking at him, not any differently that Ernest could make out, but Ernest knew that something wasn't right. "Where did you hear a thing like that?" his father said.

"I guess it was just something Uncle George said. I don't think he meant it. It was a rumor or something that somebody else had started."

"When was it?"

"Oh, a long time back. Last summer. I can't even remember for sure."

54

"Uncle George made the statement that your grandfather had been a deserter?"

"No, what he meant was that somebody else had said it, I think. He didn't say it himself, he was just reporting what someone else had said. I knew it wasn't true."

"But you asked me was it true," his father said.

"I said no it wasn't true, was it. I didn't believe it. I knew it was all a pack of lies anyway."

"You're absolutely certain that your Uncle George made that assertion?"

"He didn't make it, Father. He was saying that somebody had got the rumor started but he didn't go along with it. I can't remember what, exactly."

"Well, perhaps Uncle George will remember."

He looked at his father and back at the monocular. It was unlike any other telescope that he had ever seen, strangely shaped and having four lenses, one of which, one of the two inside the instrument, seemed to be broken loose. Ernest could not tell the severity of his father's expression because of the way the light obscured it, coming in the window behind his father's head. He looked for markings on the leather case that held the monocular. The leather was worn and dried out in spots from age and rubbing, it was very close to being powdered leather in those places where the case was scraped or badly rubbed. The strap that was attached would hang across the shoulder and was long enough to permit the instrument to be passed on to the soldier next to you without removing it from your person. But this long umbilical-like attachment was weakened in two places and would break quite easily if pulled upon too hard.

"It ought to have some neat's foot oil put on it," Ernest said. "It looks like the telescope is broken inside. One of the lenses has shaken loose." He shook the instrument and you could hear the clicking of the lens inside.

"I think we'll have to go over to Uncle George's office and have this matter straightened out."

"It wasn't really anything, Father. I don't even think he would remember."

"That is what I want to find out for myself," his father said. "It's not good to let a thing like that spread around. I'm not going to let that kind of rumor stay alive. It's entirely baseless. Your grandfather was a proper soldier and a proud one. He was a hero in the war and that is how I want him to be remembered."

• • •

Uncle George wasn't in his office on the second floor of the Real Estate Building on Marion when

56

Ernest and the doctor got there, and his door was locked. They waited in the upstairs hallway for about ten minutes. The doctor was silent except for one remark about how good Uncle George's business had to be if he could afford to leave it without so much as a note to those who might come calling. He went to the washroom while Ernest waited on the wooden bench in the hallway.

Ernest put the monocular up to his eye and tried to see on down the hallway, but the lens that was off-center inside kept him from getting it into focus. It would have to be corrected before it got entirely loose and unmanageable. It wouldn't be possible to see clearly with it until that was corrected. Ernest heard the toilet flushing and the water of the basin running. His father, being a doctor, was always very careful in cleaning his hands of any bacteria. He came out then, his face was very reddened, and he said, "We'll wait for him downstairs."

●   ●   ●

Uncle George arrived presently and he was driving a new Westcott Six with the two spares on the back. It was a flawless beauty. Uncle George was very proud of it. He placed great value on fine cars and houses and other markings of success and progress. He also liked new and modern fur-

57

niture. He liked anything that was new and anything that was luxurious. "How do you like it, Ed?" he said to his brother.

Ed was short for Edmonds, his father's middle name. Many people called him Doc or Doctor but the family called him Ed, except that Ernest's mother sometimes called him Clarence: It was a name he did not favor.

"Here, Ed, have a look under here," George said, lifting up the hood. "Look at this new speed-variation gear. It's got a self-acting governor, you see. You can adjust the tension with this thumb-screw here. The spring regulates the engine to a normal speed, you see."

"What's that tube there, Uncle George?"

"Oh, that's the carburetor, Ernie. You see, the air and vapour ports here make the gas whirl and become well-mixed before it goes into the cylinder, so it always explodes right, you see. The compression is really something. What do you think of her, Ed? Want to take a spin out to Forest Park?"

"No, George, not today. Ernest is getting ready to visit Uncle Tyler in Kansas City. We just dropped by because we had been discussing some matters concerning the family."

"Oh. No problems, I hope."

"No, no problems. Ernest was gathering up

some of Father's old things and he wants to have them. I thought it was important that you understood."

"Oh, that's all right with me," George said. "Anything the boy would like to have, anything at all."

"No, it was important, I thought, that you understood his question about Father. Something that seemed to stick in his mind about a rumor that Father had deserted during the war. Ernest said that you might have made a remark to that effect some time ago."

George looked at Ernest and then back at the doctor. "A deserter? What, Father a deserter?" He looked back at Ernest and thought a moment. Then he said, "Why, you must mean that thing about Jepson. Was that it, Ernie? That story that Jepson had that I told you about?"

Ernest looked down at the running board of the car and said, "I guess."

"You know old Jepson, Ed. When we sold the old house to him? Shucks, he always was one to get some gossip going, you know that, and where he got that story I haven't the faintest. But I set him straight on it. That's what I told you, boy, remember?"

"Yes, sir, I remember."

"So it was Jepson, was it?" the doctor said.

"Well, that was what I told you, Ernie, the way old Jepson got that rumor started and I don't know how he came upon it, but I made it straight. You can bet I made it straight."

"Well, I don't want the boy to be thinking that."

"No, you bet we don't. It was a piece of dirty gossip and there wasn't any truth to it at all. Jepson never said no more about it, that's for sure. He matter of fact apologized, as I recollect. I told him if he ever . . . Well, I told him plenty of what it isn't necessary for Ernie here to hear."

·  ·  ·

Then before they went back home that afternoon, his father seeming satisfied, and wanting Ernest to enjoy all that they had done together— the buying of the neat's foot oil for the preservation of the leather, the wallet he would need for all the money he was going to have, the pocket knife that would come in handy anytime for any cutting he might want to do—they went together for a soda at the Oak Park Ice Cream Shop. And his father looked at him and said, "You have to carry on the family tradition, son, when your old father's not around to do it." And he looked beyond him out the window. There was a vacant, shadowed look about his aging eyes.

60

•  •  •

Many years later Ernest would learn that there might have been some truth to the story about his grandfather's desertion. But he was old enough to know that there were many so accused and it had been a foolish and a tragic mixed-up war. He never thought much about it after that, and when he thought about it, it was some memento from the past that brought it to his mind. It did not matter then in later years. The question was important when he was fourteen, on that important day to both his father and to him to see things clearly in the distance, whether past or future distance you were looking at.

•  •  •

And there was little else that mattered when his father put his arm around him, only that, and since his father had said those things to him that he had hoped to hear, even in the way he had imagined he would say them, on those nights he thought about him, and wanted his father to be the way he thought he was, he felt good about the way things went that day, knowing now that what he was going to do in life was really quite important to the man who called him "son," that yes his father truly wanted him to know it was important, in that his father loved him.

# NINE (1 9 1 4)

He was avoiding going back home that Saturday morning. He knew that they were going to punish him. He had left the house early in the morning to deliver the *Oak Leaves*. It was the job he had on the weekends, taking over Thexton's paper route. He had to get up at four-thirty on that Saturday morning to deliver the village paper. His parents were still in bed when he left the house and he was careful not to wake them. But they were going to give him hell when he got back, and now when he was done with his delivery of the last paper at the last house on Van Buren Street he knew that he would not be going back home.

Not right away he wouldn't. This was his first day home since Wednesday night. They had sent the forest rangers out looking for them Thursday night. As soon as all three of them were missed, their parents sent the forest rangers out to look for them. The crutty rangers never would have found him, he knew the Preserves much better than any forest cop, and Lew and Samps went right along with him on where to go and how to elude the rangers. They were tougher than the rangers and they stuck together like the three of

62

them were one. They really had the crutty rangers running.

Well, now it was his parents who were stuck as one on this one and they were going to give him some rubbing down for it. It was even possible that his father would bring out the razor strop. Well, he would stay away as long as possible and consider the alternatives to going home. There were no alternatives that he could think of but there was always the possibility that his parents would cool down. Then, he thought, there wasn't much in that and they were going to let him have it, that was sure; and now it was a question of how tough they would be and how and whether he was going to take it off of them again. There was no choice on this one, he had come to that conclusion. There was just a chance and that a vague one that sometime later in the day they would find themselves somehow involved in something else and calming down.

So he went to the Scoville library and he sat there reading for a couple hours until he got to thinking that he had no further choice to make nor any other way to go. He would have to face them now and take it, whatever it was going to be.

And as he thought of this and how he might defend himself, he read the stories by Lieutenant Colonel J. H. Patterson, the east African adventurer, of heroic encounters with the man-eaters of Tsavo. "Pools of blood," Patterson wrote, "marked those halting places where the lion indulged in the man-eater's habit of licking the skin off so as to get at the fresh blood. This custom was confirmed by the two half-eaten bodies which I rescued: the skin was gone in places and the flesh looked dry, as if it had been sucked. On reaching the spot where the body had been devoured, a dreadful spectacle presented itself. The ground all round was covered with the blood and morsels of flesh and bones, but the unfortunate *jemader's* head had been left intact, save for the hole made by the lion's tusks on seizing him, and lay a short distance away from the other remains, the eyes staring wide open with a startled, horrified look in them. It was the most gruesome sight I have ever seen. I vowed then and there that I would spare no pains to rid the neighborhood of the bloodthirsty brutes."

Ernest became so absorbed in the narrative that he forgot about the problems that he faced. He read every page of the long account and some of them more than once. The stories were truly vivid and he did not want to leave Scoville without having read and lived reasonably each and every episode.

He hoped someday that he would be able to write like Patterson about the lions. Someday, he hoped, he would have the experiences that Colonel Patterson had to write about. He was looking forward to that and for the moment nothing else, least of all now was he looking forward to the showdown with his parents. He wasn't looking forward to that at all. But why should he be fearful of his parents just because he took a little two-day run up through the forest preserves? Colonel J. H. Patterson would have approved.

The Colonel would say that it was good for a boy of his strength and spirit to get out and lead his companions along the paths to great adventure. He would tell them that he merely wanted Lew and Sampson to learn what his own resourceful father had taught him. He would tell them that he hadn't had a chance to live a life like that of Colonel Patterson and must prepare for it by learning to survive out on his own. It would be his preparation for the time when he too would go to Tsavo to rid the neighborhood of the brutish man-eaters.

But in the end he did not tell them that. Or about the teaching Hal and Clarahan what his father had taught him. He told them none of that, and nothing else in fact that really mattered very much.

As he left the Scoville Institute and began the long walk home he thought only about the man-eaters. He walked down Grove and went on west to Kenilworth and north to Iowa. Along the way he saw the man-eaters lurking behind the trees. He narrowed his sights on them and got them right between the eyes, one, two, three. And at the camp that night the natives applauded him and staged a ceremonial dance and filled his hands with diamonds and offered him exotic native women with bare, pointed breasts who knelt in front of him and kissed his feet and hands. They set in front of him the heads of the many lions he had killed.

But all of that was gone like wisps of smoke when he walked into the house. He forgot the lions and the native women and he told his parents none of it. It was a wisp of smoke that floated off like something in a vision or a dream. He said nothing. It was a two-hour inquisition that followed fast upon his walking into the house. Nor did he mention Colonel Patterson or anything else that had anything at all to do with the good life of adventure and the hunt.

The only thought he had that had the remotest connection with Tsavo and his parents was the thought that they were man-eaters like the lions he had read about. That did occur to him a couple times during the two-hour lecture on the imperatives of right behavior, dignity and truth. He thought at the start and at the end of all of it that here was something that merited consideration. Yes, he thought as they told him what *he* was, his parents were brutish man-eaters. Very well, they told him what *he* was. Then what were they? All the time he had been thinking that he was a man. His parents did not hold that view. Well, then, what were *they*? If he was what they thought he was and said he was, then they were what he thought *they* were.

It was just a pity that Colonel J. H. Patterson was not around to rid the neighborhood of them.

# TEN (1913)

He wished that he was there. There was no other way quite like it. There was no silence like that silence anywhere. The silence of the woods, the solitary quiet no one knew, on which no sound intruded. The silence would be there with you alone and knowing of yourself. Great sheeted shafts of sunlight and of prism colours filled the clearing. In between the trees he walked upon the damp and needled twig-cushioned forest floor into the woods deep into the silence of the woods.

"I'll be right back." His father's voice.

The telescope was large. It had a barrel like a cannon that went on for miles. Looking through his end of it, he felt protected from the distant hooded monks. The lens through which their figures passed was smoked up like a piece of isinglass. He could not identify their faces then, but later saw and recognized his mother, hooded like the others, moving in procession through the scene.

The sickness in his head whirred in the night, a wind-blown picture book inside his brain of terror-ridden images. He was sweating from the sickness and the medicines. The telescope was not

68

what wakened him, it was something else, he re-called it truly, vividly when he half-wakened when they pulled him up. There was the silence of the woods. The monks moved through an archway to a chambered recess where the ceiling was high-vaulted and the air smelled dank.

He was standing in the center of the room. His hands were bound behind him. He wore a night-shirt that extended to his knees. The cord that bound his hands extended far above him to a pulley on an arch. The sunlight filled the vaulted clearings with sheeted shafts of light. Flaming smoking braziers lighted up the corners of the room. A ghostly shrieking echoed from a distant chamber of a woman being tortured. Then his mother took her place up on the platform high above the floor, sitting with the others, with the hooded Bishop and the other masked Inquisitor. She wore a mask of black, her hood was gone, she wore a long black gown. She turned to hear the Bishop whisper, "Confess."

"Strip him of his shirt," the Bishop said.

"First degree?" his mother then inquired.

"One hundred three," the Bishop said.

The hooded Executioner stood beside him and a little to one side. The Bishop nodded and the Executioner drew back on the rope, pulling it

69

and baring his teeth the way a dog does. Ernest screamed and saw the Bishop smiling. Then he went up to the ceiling, swinging, hanging there, the harsh cord biting into his wrists. Then suddenly he dropped. He seemed to faint; he realized that he was suspended only inches from the floor.

Then he stood upright but his legs were wobbly. He felt the blood that trickled down his wrists into his hands. "Second degree," the Bishop said. "Let us question him," his mother said commandingly. "Who were the first?"

Ernest said, "The Evangelicals." The Bishop nodded, smiling. "Yes," his mother smiled. He knew that he was right. He said, "They were the first to build a church in Oak Park."

"Flog him," snarled the Bishop.

"Wait, wait," said Ernest.

"Oak Park?" his mother said.

"I meant Oak Ridge, you know I did," he said. The Bishop smiled, nodding to the man who held the whip. The flogger's arm came down, the whip lay on the floor. Ernest told them everything. "1867 was when they built their church. Ontario, I think, just north of Lake."

"Flog him."

"No, that was it! It was, I'm sure of it." And he went on quickly, a great torrent of words flowing

70

out of him. "The Congregationalists it was who built the large white stone church that still remains. Then the Methodists went building on the corner of Lake and Forest, then the Unitarians and Universalists got together and then they too did build, every one of them, on the west side of Wisconsin, it was 1883. The Presbyterians moved to a building on the south side of Lake in 1886, and then the Episcopalians on Forest . . ." He went on with it, though it was muddled in his mind and came out gibberish. But then he stopped.

The Bishop was his father! Now he saw his face and yes it was his father and he calmed down then, he knew his father would show mercy. His father and his mother whispered back and forth and then his mother said, "What say you, your Eminence?"

"Infundin," said his father. "Hypoloid infundin strophantus mea."

"But your Eminence," his mother said, "he knows his churches well."

His father's mouth, angular, stern and taut; his eyes without the mask were like black marbles and there was no mistaking their stern and piercing look. Ernest was uncertain then, uneasy, and he listened to his father speak and trembled when he heard, "The boy is septicaemic. Hypoloid nux

71

vomica. Colocynth et memorized. Mea culpa cata-
pulta. Colchincinae permanganate."

"Might that be pomegranate, Clarence?" his
mother inquired.

"It's permanganate," his father said with authority. "Take the razor strap to him."

"No," Ernest pleaded.

"May we use the hairbrush?" said his mother.

"Surely, Gracie, if you think that's best," his father said, his voice and manner changing from the
stern commanding tone to meek and fawning ser-
vility. Ernest felt much better, his mother was on
his side.

He was walking deep into the silence of the
woods. "I place myself upon the mercy of the
court," he said.

His father held the razor strap above his head.
Ernest's skin was wet and clammy underneath his
shirt, and sweat dripped down his arm in back of
him and mixed with blood that dripped from off
his wrists. His hands were cupped behind him and
the blood and sweat were mixed and overflowing
from his hands. He felt weakened and his legs
began to buckle under him. His father held the
razor strap aloft. They were going to the second
degree, he knew they were, it was the water torture where they held your body in a trough and

turned a crank and stuffed a towel inside your mouth and nostrils and dripped the water on the towel until you choked. Sometimes they used a funnel in your mouth. He would confess. "Yes," he shouted to them, "yes!"

"Question him," ordered someone on the platform. It was the Inspector General, Torquemada. He had been responsible for the execution of 6,000 high school boys.

"Who was the founder of Oak Park?" the Bishop asked.

"Oak Ridge, begging your pardon's eminence."

His father smiled, turning to his mother. "The boy's a bright one. He's got a head on his shoulders. He's going to go someplace."

"Joseph Kettlestrings," Ernest answered. "It was he who founded the village of Oak Ridge. 1833. Eighteen people, Uncle George was thirty-three. They had a saw mill on the river. Then in 1837 he bought the quarter section bound by where Oak Park Avenue and Harlem meet. I know."

"The boy knows plenty for his age. I'll take him out to see the mounds."

"Not today. Let him answer this. 1870?"

"Houses built then," he answered her. "Five or six of them. West side, Avenue, Lake, the Gale house in 1867."

"Good," she said. "Now speak of the mother of churches."

It was not an easy one. He searched his mind for the answer. His English teacher, Mr. Platt, sat up on the platform waiting for his answer.

He got it then, he spoke rapidly, slurring every word, "There was a building put up in 1855 lot loaned by Mr. Kettlestrings that was called the Mother of Churches it was a schoolhouse first and then a study hall and then a Sunday school, a . . . then it was . . ." He couldn't recall.

"Never use that word again," his father said. "Wash out his mouth with the soap."

"No, wait," his mother said. "Let him speak of the Halls."

"Why not? Tell of the Hemingways, boy."

"The Halls," his mother insisted.

"Of course, the Hemingways," his father held the razor strap.

"Well, Anson," Ernest said, observing that his mother had nodded to his Eminence, but with a smile of sinister triumph, "he being your father, your Eminence, was from Plymouth, Connecticut."

"Spell it," his father said.

"The boy can't spell," Professor Platt said.

"Flog him," said his father.

"Wait," he said, "and hear me out. His father,

let me tell you what he was, and then you know I
have such trouble spelling anyway. Don't confuse
me, his father, he was here in 1852. Spit on your
shoe. Your father, your Eminence, had a dream,
and he was very religious, he knew Dwight Moody,
he worked for the YMCA, and had yourself, your
Eminence, and three other holy sons and two
daughters and they were very very poor. But
Grandfather went to real estate, for Uncle George,
and you became a doctor, like your brother, who
is very very rich, and he had a gray beard and
came from Jacob who was in the Revolution, but
Ralph begat Jacob, did he not, who came from
close the door in 1634 and went to Massachu-
setts."

"Spell it."

"I can't spell it."

"Flog him."

"The boy can't spell," Professor Platt remarked.

"I know the place, however," Ernest said. "I
know the very place."

"Well, then," said his father. "It was Blueberry,
wasn't it?"

"Begging the pardon of your Eminence, it was,
sir, Duxbury."

His father turned to his mother and said, "The
boy's got a head on his shoulders. He's going to
go someplace."

75

"He needs more practice on the cello."

"I'll take him to the mounds."

"Not unless he ceases his association with that rowdy Pentecost."

"Jack Pentecost—your Eminence—it is a holy name, as was the name of Hemingway at Yale, that being he who first went there, whose name was never told me, though I know grandmother, Anson was a hero in the Civil War, and you attended Rush, you took me there, remember, in Chicago, when old Doc Lewis told you grow a beard to make the people think all doctors who wore beards were wise. I know you wise, your Eminence, and would you have been a good geologist my friends are of that opinion, sir, what with your Smoky Mountain wisdom and your beard. Was the mountain lion big? How did you name your rifle, your Eminence? 'Old Ed.' Was that it?"

"You take me back," his father said, closing his eyes.

"Grandfather Anson told me back when he was fighting . . ."

"The Halls," his mother said.

"No, wait," his father said, raising his hand in a gesture of blessing. And then, as he began, he closed his eyes and put his head back against the cushioned headrest of the chair and said, "You take me back, there were the four of us, up in the Smokies, don't you see, and we were running out of food. We knew the people there, of course, and they were hardy mountaineers. I went out, they would not sell us food, don't you see, and saw the bees that day so that I knew there was a store of honey. I took my old felt hat. I wet it down. I lined it very carefully with leaves, the leaves I wetted in a creek around the bend, and placed small twigs and grass on top and it was very dry, don't you see, so that I lit it with a match and held this smudgepot on a branch until the bees were numbed. I seized upon the honey comb and put it in my shirt. I had to escape from there, of course, before the bees revived. At camp we used the partridge and the squirrels and cut them into little pieces and we fried them carefully and well and then I made the biscuits and I baked them on the bent sheet iron and the meat in corn meal and I fried all that in bacon drippings, don't you see. Well, they were astonished, I can tell you that, they were absolutely stunned that here old Ed had baked a truly splendid-tasting blackberry pie. The honey was what made it, don't you see. I rolled the crust dough with a beer bottle, would you be-lieve it?"

"Your Eminence did not drink the beer," his mother said. "You must make a point of that, dear."

"Dear, I poured beer out, of course I poured it out. I never drink, I never drink."

"His Eminence would never drink," she said to Ernest.

"There is a right and wrong," his father said.

"Yes, your Eminence," he said.

"Your Eminence is right," his mother said.

"You can't go wrong if you're right," the Bishop said.

"His Eminence is always right," she said.

"Now," the Bishop said, "let us assume that you are prepared to confess."

"I do confess," he said.

"Go to your room, then."

"Yes, sir."

"Wait. Flog him."

"No. What did I do wrong?"

"Flog him."

"No, what wrong did I, your Eminence?"

"Flog him."

"No. No, no, no. I confess."

"He confesses," said his mother.

"I do confess," he said. "I did it. We did it. It was wrong. They did it too. We were wrong. I

78

never meant to. It was his fault. I confess. I didn't
mean to hurt him. I confess. They made me do it.
It was wrong."

"On your knees."

"Yes, your mother's right."

"On your knees and beg the Lord's forgiveness."

He got down on his knees. His legs were weakened and the pine needles on the floor cut into
his knees. "Say you were a shameful boy," his
mother ordered.

The rope pulled at his wrists. His wrists were
bleeding, and the sweat was pouring down his
arms and mixing with the blood. He felt it drip
down drop by drop into the pool of other drops
and then he heard the sound it made of dripping
in the cups he made out of his hands behind his
back. Drip, drop, drip. He knelt before his mother
then and prayed. "Almighty God, I am ernestly
sorry that I struck my brother and I beg the
Lord's forgiveness for the locking Sis up in her
room and for the hiding it and beg the Lord to
bless them, all my sisters and my brother and my
father and my Abba Hall and Anson and my un-
cles Will and Alfred and my Uncle George and
Nanny Lily and this house and father in his wisdom and her mercy and my mother's—"

"Enough," his father cried. "I've had just about

enough. I've had much more than any one man can endure."

"We simply will not tolerate this kind of conduct," said his mother. And his father and the flogger went to work on him. He started screaming and he stopped and looked up at the wall. He felt of the wetness of his shirt. "I'll be right back," he heard. He felt dizzy and his body trembled. At his back, beyond the window shade, there was a brightness. He turned carefully and reached back for the shade and pulled it up. The sill was wet. The rain had come in through the slightly opened window. The dawn was brightening the sky. On the table at the side of the bed were medicines he hadn't seen the night before.

His father's voice—"I'll be right back." Outside the room. Going on down the stairs. Ernest sat up in the bed. He felt weakened. He looked straight ahead, staring at the wall, and saw the shadows that the light cast of the droplets of the rain upon the window. He was walking in the woods.

In between the trees he walked upon the damp and needle twig-cushioned forest floor into the woods deep into the silence of the woods. Great sheeted shafts of sunlight and of prism colours filled the clearing. The silence would be there with you alone and knowing of yourself. The silence

80

of the woods, the solitary quiet no one knew, on
which no sound intruded. There was no silence
like that silence anywhere. There was no other
way quite like it. He wished that he was there.

## ELEVEN (1916)

Marion Lambert, murdered or a suicide, hadn't been much older than his eldest sister, Marcelline. Marce—known as Maaz and Ivory too to him, for reasons of his own invention—watched baby Les that night. The other sisters gathered in his room. It was the year they talked about the murder.

It was a year when anti-Kaiser jokes were popular, and when the puns on soldiers and sailors were the rage ("Beat the tar out of the sailor? No, I had him arrested for assault.") None of the jokes was popular for long, the laughs were getting longer though, the war was on and everything was changing fast.

Other headlines, other stories, made the papers thicker. Chicago papers told of photoplays that would be getting out to Forest Park before they reached Oak Park. Mabel Normand's face appeared on posters everywhere. One vied for attention near the Warrington on Wisconsin Avenue, the Warrington being a legitimate theatre where prices now were down to half as much as those of photoplays (75 cents would buy the best seat in the house), and Griffith was the big name in the motion pictures then, with Evelyn Nesbit in the papers once again when all that happened was eleven years ago, saying she would be a motion picture star as well, it was reported.

In politics that year the rule that was the safest, what they said, was tie up with the man who would do business at the drop of a hat and not who wants to sleep on it. And Ernest read Flo Ziegfield's name and thought he was a woman. Ziegfield said *Canary Cottage* proved that Cantor ought to be with Fields and the cowboy named Will Rogers in the Follies. The Follies never got to Oak Park, Illinois. George M. Cohan did once though, and then Caruso's voice without Caruso, auditioned by their mother on the Grafonola. It was a recording called *Questa o quella*, H.M.V. No. 81205. She *said* it was Caruso.

His voice then, and the Maxwells and electric suction sweepers got to Oak Park, Illinois, along with news about the murder of the Lambert girl. Their mother told his sisters always to be careful coming home, and never go alone into Chicago, for whatever reason. What reason would they have, unless to see Theodosia Goodman in the vampire photoplay, the Theodosia "Theda" now, the Goodman "Barranger" and the Barranger "Bara." Everything was changing overnight.

The murder happened in Wisconsin anyway, or near the border of the states: Lake Forest, Illinois, in fact, that was, their mother said, almost as respectable as Oak Park; then, after that discussion, she was disinclined to talk beyond the point of warning by that one example of the girl—murdered or a suicide—who wasn't much older than his eldest sister Marcelline.

• • •

Maaz was looking after Les that night. Les was one year old. They called him "Gaspipe" and "The Pest." The other girls were up in Ernest's room. "I think the girl was murdered," Ernest said.

Ursula sat on the floor with Carol.

Sunny sat on the corner of the bed on which he stretched himself, his head resting on the pillows. The chair next to the desk went unoccupied. Their parents had gone off to a meeting of the Anti-Saloon League in the village, leaving him and Maaz in charge.

"Her father found the footprints of the guy," he said.

"The paper said she didn't think life was worth living," Sunny said. "And that she said that she was queer herself."

"Don't you know anything, Nunbones?" he looked down the bed at her. "If I held my shotgun to your head and said you better write what I told you, would you do it?"

84

"Don't say that," she said and shivered. Her big brown eyes were like polished agates and her face all white.

"Maybe she didn't know it was cyanide," said Ursula.

"And where'd she get it?"

"I mean, the man *could* have told her it was something else."

"Good thinking. Old Uralegs is on the right track, girls."

"I wish Maaz would come," said Carol.

"Don't call me that," Ursula said to Ernest.

"What, you scared or something?" Ernest said to Carol.

"I don't like to hear about it," Carol said. She was the youngest of the sisters.

"Don't call me Uralegs."

"Well, maybe Beefie better leave," he said. "I don't want her yapping to you know who."

"Go find Maaz," Sunny told her.

"I'm afraid."

"Well, don't then," Sunny said. "Stay here and be afraid."

"There's no reason to be afraid," he said. "Not unless they got the wrong guy. Then we all got to worry. But old Doc Webster clinched it when he testified. He went to Rush Medical."

"Does father know him?"

"No, he don't know him. But he told me that Doc Webster proved that the spots on the girl's coat were cyanide and had to be a liquid."

"What does that mean?"

"Don't interrupt," he said. "Why didn't the undertaker show the spots to the Coroner when he found them?"

"What's a Coroner?"

"Why didn't he? Well, maybe because he was in on it. So Orpet went on back and got the bottle and he spilled the stuff on Marion's coat."

"Who's Orpet?"

"Quiet, Beefie," Ursula said.

"That's too complicated," Sunny said.

"Well, Maaz can tell you," Ernest said. "She agrees with me that Orpet killed the girl."

"I wish Maaz would come."

"Quiet."

"My theory is that they were sweethearts all along. He admitted that. Then he said he lied. He said he bought the bottle too."

"But the bottle was empty," Ursula said.

"Oh, you know all about it, I guess," he said.

"No, but he said he filled the bottle with molasses."

"Well, if that was it, why did he lie about it?"

"I don't know," she said.

"Anyway," he said, "they found the bottle."

"They did?" Sunny asked.

"Sure they found it. And it had molasses in it."

"Then he *was* telling the truth," Ursula said.

Ernest glared at her. Marcelline came in then saying, "Well, the Pest's asleep. Finally." She sighed and sat down in the chair by the desk. "What's everybody so quiet for?"

"It's scary," Carol said.

Ernest, lying back on the bed, explained, "We're talking about the Lambert case. They think Orpet's innocent."

"I don't," Sunny said.

"I do," Ursula said.

"I do too," Beefie said.

"You do too?" Ernest laughed. "You don't even know who Orpet is. You don't even know what a prosecutor is."

"What is it?"

"Never mind," he said. "You tell them, Maaz. You think Orpet did it, don't you?"

"Well," she said, "it was established that the poison in the greenhouse wasn't potassium cyanide but sodium. That made Doctor Webster's testimony useless."

"Doesn't Father know him?" Ursula asked.

"But look at the other testimony of the other druggist," Ernest said. "Orpet bought two cans of cyanide from *him*."

"But they were never opened," Marcelline said. "They were for his father."

"Oh, sure, they were for his father, sure. Well, that's plenty hard to prove."

"You ought to be a lawyer, Ernie," Ursula said.

"Yeah, well maybe I will," he said.

"I'm sleepy," Beefie said.

"Go to bed then," Sunny said.

"Yes, go to bed," Marcelline told her. "This isn't a proper subject for you to hear, anyway."

"I'm scared."

"Well, let's change the subject and have some games, Old Brute. Leave it to the jury."

"Juries make mistakes sometimes," he said.

"Oh, I don't know about that," she said.

"Well, how about the Hallawall case, then?" He just made up the name Hallawall, looking out through the open door, and then he invented a long complicated story, hoping to frighten them a little: It involved a jury on which the actual murderer was serving. He ended it with, "And so Hallawall told the other members of the jury that *he* was the guilty one. And, because of his honesty, they never turned him in."

They all fell for it, except Marcelline. But by
the time he finished, Carol was asleep, her head
resting in Ursula's lap. Ursula yawned.

"I hope I'm not keeping anyone awake," he said.

"No, go on, I'm interested," Sunny said.

"Well, there isn't much more to tell, except that
Hallawall, the killer, is right out here now in Oak
Park."

Marcelline laughed.

Ursula, suddenly wide awake, said, "Where?"

"Over at the Elmwood Garage. That's right, he's
a mechanic over there. He still has the old wrench
he used to kill the guy. He showed it to me. It's
got the blood stains on it and everything. He was
working on a roadster and he pulled the wrench
out of his back pocket and he showed it to
me."

"Golly," Sunny said.

"Why don't you turn him in?" Ursula wanted
to know. "You could be a hero."

"I intend to," Ernest said. "I'm absolutely going
to turn him in. It's my bounden duty as a citizen.
After all, he admits to killing Fawkes. I might
turn him in tomorrow. No, I think I'll wait."

"Why wait?" Ursula said.

"Why not?" he said. "I'll wait till Guy Fawkes
Day." He laughed. He laughed so much he shook

the bed. Carol woke up. His other sisters laughed. Carol didn't know what it was about.

They heard the door downstairs and quieted. "You better scat," he said to the girls. "Go on, get out of here. The Old Physician's home."

• • •

It was the year the Follies picked up Cantor and the Goldwyn Company came into being to make more photoplays and Mabel Normand had her picture on the posters by the Warrington.

William Orpet, on July 15th that year, was acquitted of the charge of murder in the death of one Marion Lambert. The case remained a mystery.

# TWELVE (1915)

The heavy snow that was forecast for the game with Thornton did not arrive; nor did the victory predicted for Thornton. The final score was Oak Park 46, Thornton 10.

Ernest and the others were kept out of it. They were from the Minors. The game with Thornton was on the Majors' schedule. The Majors were the heavyweights and he and Bell and Golder, Janotta, Gordon and Fox, were lightweights. The Minors' scrimmages preceded all the Majors' games, that was the rule, but they were changing that, or moving toward a change, and there had been a special understanding for this game. Still, the Minors warmed the bench and waited, hoping Hanna would be big enough to let them play.

Hanna, who was the Manager for the heavyweights, saw that Ernest and the other Minors stayed on the bench. Then there was Boyle at the end of the bench, getting up and down and pacing back and forth, as if he worried that *his* team was out there on the field losing. Boyle was the Minors' Manager. His boys were sitting back and losing on the bench. That was the way *he* played the game. And it was the Thornton team that was out there losing anyway, so neither Boyle nor Hanna had any excuse not to let them see some action.

Boyle looked at Hanna. Possibly he was thinking, Why don't you let my boys get in and run it up for you?

Possibly, very probably, Hanna was a bastard.

Ernest felt that way and maybe Boyle was of that opinion too. He ought to be, being as his team had made this trip to get the workout that would back them up for Riverside and Marshall and—Thanksgiving Day—that all-important final game at Princeton, Illinois.

Being too as his team had beaten Proviso. Ernest hadn't done too bad in that one, nor had Fox, Golder, Janotta, Bell or Gordon. But maybe Hanna hadn't heard about that game, and maybe Boyle had forgot. And maybe Hanna, having heard about it, got a little envious and was holding back because of that.

Boyle, Ernest thought, why don't you tell him? Ernest watched the Majors romp all over Thornton for the first and almost all the second quarter, then he turned to Golder and he said what was it.

"Hell, we could be standing still out there and win," his teammate said.

"Don't I know it."

Fox was sitting on the other side of Golder and he said, "Hanna's just being a hog about it. He thinks he's Zuppke."

"Well, Zuppke would have let us in," said Golder.

"Well, Boyle ought to push him," Ernest said.

"Boyle, who's he?" Golder said. The sarcasm was written all over his face and he looked on down the bench at Boyle. Golder made a profane remark concerning Boyle.

Ernest said it too. "Twice," he said.

"Why doesn't Elton tell him?" Fox said.

Elton was the Captain of the Majors. "He's another one," Golder said.

"Him too," Ernest said, meaning the profanity. Well he was going to put it up to Boyle at the halftime.

Then he went to Boyle at the half. He said that he was speaking for himself and all the Minors on the bench. He put it up to him as reasonably as he could and Boyle looked at him and said, "What's eating you guys, anyway? Hanna either does it or he don't. It ain't the rule, you know. There's nothing says he has to. You got no cause to get spiteful, Hemingway. You're all acting like a pack of amateurs."

Ernest went back and sat down on the bench

and looked at Boyle. The Majors had a lead already of some 20 points, it was just a scrimmage, and they, the Minors, were not getting into it. They had John Marshall coming up. They had a victory string already going for them. They could have used this game to toughen up for Marshall. But Boyle thought that they were amateurs. He was one hell of a Manager, all right.

• • •

But in the second half, Boyle talked to Hanna. Hanna looked on down the bench at them. That's all he did, he looked down at them. And shook his head.

"Steen, what did Boyle say?"

"What do you think he said? Look at him." Boyle was backing off from Hanna. Hanna was shaking his head while Boyle backed away and looked out to the field.

"He said we was a pack of animals, if you want to know," Ernest said.

"What?" Fox said.

"Hell, they're only going to win this one by 40 points."

• • •

But when the season ended they, the Minors, were the victors. They ran their victory string to seven. There was only one game that they lost. In

94

points, they racked up 183 against the 53 for their opponents.

It ended with the Majors losing three of their big games.

The Minors were the Suburban League Champions. The Majors were nothing, unless there was a title that they gave you for third place.

• • •

So he and Fox and Golder got together at the season's end. They met on Saturday afternoon when there was no game or any other thing they had to do. It was a cold day and they took a long walk out to Forest Park. They might get lucky at Servito's tavern. The village of Oak Park was without taverns since old Holy Henry closed them up back in 1868. There were three saloons on Lake Street then and Henry Austin came along and bought them up and poured the whiskey out into the street. Then he pushed his righteous resolutions through that kept the village dry.

So they got together then, the three of them, and went out west to what had been once known as Harlem. They stood outside Servito's in the starting snow and coming wind. The snow came down in flurries as they hung around outside and watched.

They had to be on guard against Oak Parkers

coming by and seeing them go in. Oak Parkers did not drink or smoke. They did not patronize Servito's. That included them: They were going to make themselves an exception. When the coast was absolutely clear, they were going to go on in and drink and smoke like Forest Parkers and the other world outside Oak Park.

They waited and they watched. The wind was starting up and it was getting colder. Ernest tried to peer inside Servito's window. It was frosted over. He could see a light inside that looked opaque but saw his face reflected too and thought at first it couldn't be him, it looked in some way fierce. The image in the glass was like the face he'd seen once on a trapper up in Michigan who used to talk to animals. He kicked his feet against the brickwork below the window and he heard Lloyd Golder say, "How about it, Steen? We were right, weren't we, Hemingsteen? God damn it, we were right."

Ernest grinned and looked at his reflection in the glass. He liked the way old Golder swore. They were going to drink and smoke and swear, the way the world outside the village drank and smoked and swore; the way a few of other, older villagers were known to do, the ones who did what was not talked about to them; the way the Wops did and the other outsiders who passed on through the village on their sober way to Forest Park and on their drunken way on back at 4 a.m., escorted by the Keystone Cops; the way the others, better ones, were known to do; done by some, but not by them; by others of their age, but not by them.

"That God damn Hanna had a great season, didn't he boys?" Golder's voice was shaky, he was that cold.

Fox laughed. "What was it Detroit beat him?"

"Hell, 39 to 7," Golder said. "Something kind of onesided, you might say."

"What?" Fox said.

"We ought to send him clips from the paper," Golder said. "How'd you like to see his face with him reading all about the champs of the suburb league?"

"That's *us*," Fox shouted into the cold gray air, and then he roared with laughter and they all laughed then and Golder stomped his feet against the walk and spat out on the street.

"Whataya say, Hemingsteen? You think Servito might be ripe enough to give the suburb-league champs a couple snorts?" Golder slapped him on the back. Ernest turned and grinned and said, "Hell, it's worth a try."

"Whataya say?" Fox said.

97

Ernest liked the standing there with the wind
and cold. He liked to hear old Golder swear. He
liked to know that they were champs. Well, the
champs could go inside now, there being no witnesses around, and they were cold enough to need
a drink and look like needing one. He kicked his
feet against the bricks below the window and he
saw the faces of his two companions in the glass
like in a mirror and saw the funnels of their
breaths come out their nostrils and he liked the
way it was, he liked the snow, the cold air and
the wind, the game of football and the time of
year, the getting hurt out on the field in a battle
that left you something that you had to have to
keep on holding as your own.

They were men and ought to get a drink.

"Whataya say?"

"Hell, it's worth a try," Fox said. "Who's going
to ask him?"

"Steen, who else?" said Golder.

"Yeah, Steen's got the way with words, all right,"
Fox said.

"We'll tell him Hanna sent us," Ernest said.

Fox and Golder laughed.

"That bugger," Fox said.

"Don't call him that," Ernest said.

"Yeah," said Golder, "think of something worse
than that."

Ernest said, "He's just a tough old bastard. But we'll be tougher than he is come next season."

"That's right," echoed Fox, going in last behind them through the door.

• • •

Inside it was a slow day for Servito and he gave them whiskeys if they wouldn't bring their friends in or come back when he had crowds. "Like I say," he said, "I don't want your old man coming in here with no complaints. You don't know where you got this."

They agreed that they would keep their mouths shut, which was more than others who had told *them,* and Servito sold them double-shots, at more than others paid. They drank them neat and quietly back in the corner near the door that led out to the alley.

Feeling warm and good then on their way back in the cold air and the snow that afternoon—the sky much darker now—now the wind a freezing wind—they started out to run all the way on back down Madison and over then to Lake and ran on down the brick street into town, their faces reddened from the whiskey and the cold. And Ernest looked at Golder and at Fox and saw their breaths and thought of horses he remembered snorting in the cold air of a winter morning after early dawn.

Feeling very good and drunk they ran on down the brick streets of the village shouting vile epithets about the schools that they would fight and beat next year. Like horses running in the cold crisp air in snow and wind on that November afternoon when next year's football lay ahead and last year's games were fading memories at season's end.

## THIRTEEN (1915)

The night that Dr. Willoughby Hemingway, Ernest's physician-missionary uncle, gave his lecture on China at the Third Congregational Church, Ernest was required to attend.

Uncle Willoughby had been honored by the governor of Shansi for having stopped the spread of the bubonic plague in that northern Chinese province. Ernest had heard it all before at the house and at the school. This would be the third time. Savage, Blount and Lockyer were all going down into the "skin-n-sin" levee district of Chicago and he hated missing that. He would hear about it second-hand. But Uncle Will was lecturing and he was obliged to attend.

He had to wear the faded maroon tie with the fleurs-de-lys on it. He had to wear the shiny dark suit that was too short in the pants; he had to wear the brown shoes that were too tight at the toes. He hated the tie and the shoes and the suit that was just a hand-me-down. But he had to wear it. He hated the Third Congregational Church as well, as the First and the Second, but that was all another story. What he really hated was the required part.

It was the lantern-slide lecture on China. He had heard it all before. He liked the part that sounded like Angus Hamilton's Afghanistan. He liked the words that Hamilton had written about the weekly markets that were held upon the plains just east of town where all of the roads converged, where throngs of Persian carts arrived, where ill-fed baggage horses came along burdened down with all they were obliged to bear, where gurgling camels spat on the natives: He liked all that, and all the intrigue of the market place—everything that he would like to see first-hand to talk and write about the way his uncle talked about the places he had known first-hand. But that was not what his uncle talked about this night, and Ernest did not listen very carefully.

He listened or pretended to, the way his mother expected of him, and he was well-behaved. They were in the sixth pew back, his parents and his sisters and himself, and he sat pretending while he thought about the other things: Afghanistan, the girls who sat in front of him, and what Savage, Blount and Lockyer might be up to. They would have a great time and he wished that he was with them to laugh it up and roughhouse the way they did whenever they escaped. He was imprisoned in this church where his mother often sang and his father always listened, or pretended. He pretended too.

•   •   •

Uncle Will had taught him many things about the Chinese. He had explained the characters that were their alphabet and symbols of ideas. It started with the simple shape of objects and the sounds applied to many things. Like the word for horse— "*Ma* is horse." But *ma* could also be "mother" so that woman-horse became mother, and jade-horse was agate, and insect-horse became locust.

Uncle Will also told Ernest of the five bats, or *wu fu,* that are often painted on Chinese plates. They represented the five blessings, "longevity, wealth, *mens sana in corpore sano,* love of virtue, and a peaceful end." And why did they call them "bats" Ernest wanted to know. "Because the character of bat is identical in sound with that of 'blessing.'" Did he understand?

Ernest always said he understood. He liked his uncle's stories of the secret sects, of Pwan-Koo, of sleeve dogs and the like. There were many sects. One of them was the Golden Orchid where unmarried girls agreed not to make love with their husbands after marriage. His uncle used the word "cohabit." Why did girls do that?

"It's a practice that is strictly prohibited," Uncle Willoughby said.

And Pwan-Koo, he was like our Adam, "but altogether legendary, don't you see? When he died, the work of creation began. That is what the Chinese believed. Pwan-Koo's breath became the wind, his voice became the thunder, his right eye the sun, his left the moon."

"And what became man?" Ernest wanted to know.

His uncle looked at him with his sharp and penetrating eyes and smiled. "Gracie?" he called to Ernest's mother. "Oh, Gracie."

His mother came in from the kitchen, wiping her hands on her apron. Yes, what was it? "Did you hear that question, Gracie? The boy brought up an extraordinary question. How did man come about, he asked. In the Chinese legend of Pwan-Koo, you see." And then he turned to Ernest and explained, "Man, according to the legend, came from the parasites that infested Pwan-Koo's body. Now you can understand why I have to bring the message of Our Lord and Savior Jesus Christ to them."

"Uncle Will's quite right," Ernest's mother said. She straightened her apron and walked back through the swinging doors to the kitchen.

Yes, but Ernest didn't really understand. He wanted to learn and understand, and he had taken up the practice of inquiring of the truth. On the way, he had done some things of which his parents did not approve. He had once arrived at a bitter judgment, that what the truth was to his mother was something that you had to do, of church, of music, of obedience and obligations. Uncle Willoughby was of the same opinion: He agreed with Ernest's parents. Still Ernest, at the time, did not understand about man coming from the parasites that infested Pwan-Koo's body, nor why his uncle had to bring the message of Jesus Christ to the Chinese for that reason. "I see," he said to his uncle, wanting him to tell him more about the dogs the Chinese carried in their sleeves.

• • •

The night Uncle Willoughby lectured, he called them "lion dogs" and Ernest thought of them as little lions. Then he thought about the girls who sat in front of him. His uncle talked about the family system of old China. Ernest had his mind on Angela Kaufmann. She was of a very wealthy family and her step-father was quite elderly. He would die soon and Angela would inherit a good deal of money. The Kaufmans had all of the bless-

105

ings of the Chinese bats. But Angela was too much blessed, he thought, with love of virtue.

"Custom," his uncle was saying, "obliged the son to render obedience during all of his father's lifetime."

Ernest listened but he thought about Angela Kaufmann.

"The *Li Ki* says that the son must inquire of the health of his parents and bring them water to wash and the best of food."

Ernest thought about the night he went out to start the car. His parents were asleep and he was afraid that he would wake them. But he got it started, thinking he would take it for a spin around the block, and then he turned it off. He thought he would run into trouble with it somewhere before he got it back, and they would give him holy hell. It would be as bad as when he broke the wedding vase from Nettie.

His uncle went on to talk of the need of Christian teaching in the provinces. Ernest thought about Pwan-Koo's parasites and whether the heathen Chinese that came out of them were worse than many of the self-righteous Christians who sat around him now. Betsy Popkin sat in front of him. Her father had run away with Mary Anne Dunn, his secretary.

106

"Children were to be indulged until the age of eight, when they were taught manners and the art of yielding to others."

Two years ago, his father had taught him plenty about manners after he had misbehaved at the Coliseum during the Valentine's Day party and later at the church. And he remembered when he and Samps had killed the porcupine and his father had lectured them on shooting harmless animals and made them cook and eat it. He had yielded then, and to his mother many times. Mrs. Schooler had yielded to Derek Slocum, they said, before her husband died. She wore the feather hat and ermine-collar coat that she had acquired after her husband's passing. Mary Anne Dunn had yielded.

"Hongkong, our corruption of the local pronunciation of the Chinese name, means fragrant lagoon . . . is 26 miles in circumference, and nine in length by eight in breadth . . ."

Betty Marsh was fragrant something and well worth corrupting, as Oscar Simon knew looking over at her clipped hair nestled about her Dutch-boy collar. "Escape to China, fellow villagers, the music of the bagnio lures you here, and there are words and music by degenerates, corrupting . . . The music and the demimonde of Paris demand control, the dances of the brothel tempt, the scarlet sister and her business threaten. Guard against contagion. Avoid transgressions . . ."

"So if you propose to do what is no good, only consider what it will do to disgrace the names of your father and mother." His uncle was quoting from the Chinese.

No, he would never disgrace their names, there was no fun in that. Oscar, in the second pew, disgraced by his brother's suicide that bared the family's gray insanity. Oscar had no brain to kill himself but none of those in passing would pass close enough to contract it, for his onetime welcome in the houses of the village ended with his brother's godless act. Corruption too in Velma Cheterton, the gadabout who got about too much. Ben Corson's daughter raped. The druggist's son on Marion who whirlwinded on the summer grass under the aging oak in April. All in the church-a-going village far from the heathen Chinese shores.

•   •   •

The medical-missionary uncle Reverend Doctor Willoughby Hemingway monotoned, illuminating the inscrutable, as sinners were appalled to learn the godless habits of the Orient, the eunuchs of the Empress, the abominable Chinese coroner, the grim disordered, deluded, unchristian oriental mind.

. . .

Ernest snickered thinking of Mrs. Zangwill's mustache, then coughed, looking at his mother. She gave him a stern glare of disapproval and the promise of a later word, a reprimand. Her china-blue eyes and stern locked jaw. She would never know and he would never tell her, not in a million dynasties. "Old persons," his uncle was saying, "are in authority and may be tyrants if they like. The young have very little recourse."

The Chinese were no different. Did a Chinese boy ever sneak the family ricksha for a ride around the block? Well, they needed us, all right, to show them how to use the gunpowder they invented, and some say printing and the wheel. Grim, disordered, deluded, unchristian orientals.

Later, after he had been spoken to, after getting off to bed without being sacrificed, after all his lies, he seriously considered whether God might have punished Mrs. Z. by giving her a mustache.

He liked to think there was some truth in that. In anything.

He went to sleep, dreaming of Afghanistan.

# FOURTEEN (1914)

He told his sisters to stay out. "Out of the bedroom," he told them. "And out of the basement too."

They knew he meant it, they were afraid of him. It was a reasonably respectful kind of fear in deference to his male senior status in the family. Except for Father. But there were some ways he had of keeping them in line that even Father lacked.

It was the Saturday night that the boys came for the initiation. Cusack was the first to arrive. Ernest let him in at the side door and told him to go on down into the basement. Cusack grinned his big grin and stroked his jaw and went on down. He was one of those guys who got a kick out of a setup like this.

Harry Haselton and Maury Loven came together. They were scared. They went down at his command. Cusack would take care of them. Loven had a funny haircut, Haselton was thin and pale and, as always, like they said, a little of a "Jenny Willocks." Worthington and Voelke got there right on time. "Go on down," he told them. "Haselton and Loven just got here."

•  •  •

"Ernie?" It was his sister in the hallway. The

110

lights were out but there was no mistaking who it was. Well, what'd she want? "What's going on, anyway?"

Boy, it was just like her to mess things up. "Look, just get back in the kitchen and you keep out of this. I want it dark, you understand?"

"What for?"

"Never you mind what for."

"Look, you better tell me, Ernie, or you know what . . ."

"Yeah, what?"

"You just better tell me."

"Well, if you have to know, it's for the Rifle Club. Now, damnit, Maaz, just keep out of it, you understand?"

"What're you going to do with that?"

She meant the dried porcupine skin that he was holding. "Never you mind."

"Can I watch?"

"No, you can't watch. This ain't nothing for girls. You just keep that door shut and keep your clapper shut too."

He went on down the stairs and into the basement with the others. He had the flashlight with him but he didn't turn it on until he had the porc skin hid behind the stairs. He had taken all the lights out earlier, so they were in the dark until

111

he turned the flashlight on. "Can't we have some light down here?" Cusack said.

"No, you can't," he said. Cusack was in on it, of course. "I got to go back up and let the others in. Don't make no noise."

He went back up the stairs and waited for the others to arrive. He checked to see that Maaz was in the kitchen.

She knew about the Boy's Rifle Club, all right; she knew that he had made it up. He had been writing about it in the *Trapeze,* marking meetings and the shoots and trophies, all the business they had conducted that, in fact, no one had done at all. There being a Girl's Rifle Club, not having a Boy's Rifle Club was ridiculous. That was what he had decided. Only nobody got into it for free. They had to be initiated. And everything, with his parents both away, was right for it. Tonight, downstairs, Cusack, Loven, Haselton, Sperry, Taylor, Jenkins, Voelke, Hopkins, Fisk, Coleman, Thexton, Haupt, Golder, Ellis and Pentecost—all present and accounted for.

"Where the hell is Wagenknecht?" he said.

"He and Speelman ain't coming," Golder said.

"They better come," he said. The porcupine skin was stuck away and hidden between the angled stair supports.

"You know Eddie, he don't believe in this kind of stuff."

Ernest focussed the flashlight on where the voice was coming from. It was Pentecost, of course, his hair slicked back. He had that wicked brockster look in his eyes and in the way he grinned. He was going to make it tough on the initiates.

"It's spooky down here," Loven said.

"Yeah, can't we have some light?" Haupt said.

They were two of the six initiates. Ernest crept up behind Loven and said, "How's this?" giving him the flashlight blindingly in the eyes. The knowing members laughed; the others were too scared to laugh.

"Look," he said with mock anger, "you either want to be in on this or you don't. Now, if you want some light, get out of here and go down to Popkin's with the other girls. If you can't take it and you don't want no part of this organization, I'm inviting you to leave right now."

There were no takers, they knew better than to turn tail on this one.

"I went to a lot of trouble to get you guys in this," he said. "I got a bunch of guns lined up and everything, and I got the camera for the picture so it's all set up."

"Where we going to be for that?"

"The picture? Over at the school, where else? That's where the dumb molls took theirs. We got to make it look better than they did."

He could feel the tension among them, he knew that they were scared. Too bad Wag and Speelman didn't show, he would have liked to spook the hell out of them. They were nippies, that was for sure.

"You sure McDaniel's going to let this in? I mean the picture?"

"What's he got to do with it, anyway? I'm going to make him an Honorary member." They laughed at that. Somebody asked if the picture was going to be in the *Trapeze*.

"We'll get it in the *Tabula*," he said in answer to the faceless voice.

"How?"

"I got it all set up. Don't you worry none."

"Hell, let's get on with the initiation." That was Pentecost, he knew what was coming.

"I figured we might wait for Speelman."

"Hell, he ain't coming. You know him."

"Well, he's a God damn nig-pig if he don't."

"That's okay. We got fourteen guys already, and we're going to have twice that much."

"If we get our pictures in, they're going to know who's part of it."

114

"So what?" he challenged Voelke, exposing him with the flashlight. "If we got twenty-eight guys, are they going to hang all of us?"

"That's right," Jack said.

"Where're the other guys?"

"I got them all committed, don't you worry," Ernest said.

"Sure, we don't have to worry," Cusack said.

"Let's get on with the torture," Jack Pentecost said.

Ernest, trying to sound as menacing as possible, said, "If anyone bleeds, I got my old man's alcohol and bandages."

"Boy, we're going to need them," Golder said.

"I got the *thing* all ready. It's in a double-barred cage. And let me tell you, it's as hungry as a God damn wolf."

"What is it?" Loven asked uneasily.

"Never you mind," Ernest said. "It only bites one out of every four or five, and you might be one of the lucky ones."

"Didn't it kill old man Smeeth's watchdog the other night?" Pentecost said.

"Naw, it just crippled him a little. Bit off his right front leg."

"How's he doing?"

"The dog or the *thing*?"

"Hell, I don't give a damn about the thing. I hate that Tasmanian crut."

It was pitch dark. The talk about the thing was spooking them, all right. Golder, going along with it, asked what was a Tasmanian.

"You ain't never heard of a Tasmanian devil?" Ernest asked. "Well, they say he's just about the most vicious and ugliest critter ever known. And the *thing* is even worse."

"Let's get on with it," Jack said. "My old man's waiting on me."

"If you want out, Jack, you just go right on."

"I didn't mean that," Jack said. "It's just that I can't stand thinking what might happen if the *thing* gets out with all of us in here. I don't want to end up being its God damn dinner."

"Well, I gave it a rat to eat this afternoon," said Ernest. "It can't go without food for more than half a day. It eats anything."

"Jesus," Cusack said in mock fear, "I'm scared."

"What're you scared about?" Pentecost wanted to know.

"Okay, okay. You guys line up there against the wall." He trained the flashlight on the wall and on the old skins his father had hanging there and on the cobwebs too. "You, Haupt, over there against the wall. You too, Loven. All of you, over there."

116

The initiates lined up against the wall and stood there in the darkness.

"Watch the cobwebs now. We got black widows all over the place." There *was* one that he had seen. "Okay, face the wall now. Now take your shirts off."

"What's that for?" Lyman said.

"Never you mind," he said. "It's for the *thing,* if you want to know."

"Come on, don't try to scare us with that stuff," said Voelke.

Ernest and Golder laughed. Golder said, "There ain't no reason to be scared. Unless it bites you."

"Who's going to get it out of the cage?" Pentecost asked.

"*I'm* not going to touch it," Golder said.

"I got some heavy leather gloves," said Ernest. "I forgot to put them on the other night, when I was feeding it the rats, and it like to took a bite out of my hand. It ate both the rats, gobbled 'em right up. Chewed their heads right off and spit 'em out."

"Come on," Cusack said.

"Yeah, let's get it over with," Loven said.

"You sure? I mean, you guy's ain't too scared, are you?"

No one answered him. He went back of the

117

stairway and got the porcupine skin. He made some growling noises and yelped once back in the corner. "Jesus Christ," he said. He growled again, imitating animal noises and trying to mock all of the night creatures he had ever heard. Golder said, "Jesus, Steen, be careful."

"I got the bugger by the legs," he said. "Hold still now, God damn you. I got it. Boy, is it hungry. Jesus, I hope I don't lose my hold on it."

"My God be careful," Pentecost said in a shaky voice.

"God, is it ugly," Golder said.

The members who were in on it all made horrifying noises as Ernest approached the victims with the thing. They all stood with their backs to him. They had their shirts off. "Okay, Cusack, you got to give me a hand now, it's kicking up a little. Watch out for the fangs."

And then, after keeping up a long silence, Ernest let them have it, one by one. He rubbed the sharp quills up and down Maury Loven's bare back. Loven yelled. Jack pulled him away from the others and said, "Thank God he didn't bite you. You were lucky."

Each of the others yelled out at the touch of the quills. Cusack and Golder and Pentecost pulled them back one by one. Haselton was the one who

shook the most before he got it, turning quickly,
yelping, as he felt the sharpness of the quills.
They'd all thought it was alive, of course, and
none of them had ever felt of quills before, not
on a bare back anyway.

They all laughed once it was over.

. . .

Ernest's sister Maaz came down to warn him
that their parents were back home. Ernest led the
way as they all scampered out the side door to
the alley. They gathered laughing in the back out
by the shed and all the new initiates were laughing more than the other members of the club.

"Were you scared?" Ernest asked Haupt.

"I was more scared of the spiders than the
thing," he said.

"I knew it wasn't no Tasmanian thing," Maurice
Loven said.

"Yeah, what do you know about it?" Pentecost
asked him.

"I've read about them," Maury said. "They
come from Tasmania."

"Well, ain't he smart. Hear that, guys? Maury
says Tasmanians come from Tasmania. Ain't that
brilliant?"

"Yeah, where *is* Tasmania, if you're so smart?"
Golder asked of Loven.

"Over in the Orient. Near China."

"It's in Australia, if you want to know," Ernest said.

"Well, I was scared a little," Taylor said. "I don't like spiders."

"That's what we ought to do with Speelman," Ernest said. "We ought to get him in a dark room like a closet and tell him there's a black widow in there."

"Yeah, we could get a real one, a dead one," Golder said. "Just hang him by a thread up in the closet."

"I heard this story about a guy once," Pentecost said, "when they locked him up in a room with a corpse. It was all crippled and mangled up in an accident with a farm machine, see, and this guy was in the room with it and he lit a match and saw the corpse sitting there. Well, he's supposed to have broke the God damn door down getting out."

"Jesus," Voelke said.

They were all quiet for the moment, thinking. "That's a hell of a story," Ernest said. Then they started laughing once again, thinking of the porc and all.

Ellis scratched a lot, he had a tender skin.

•   •   •

FOURTEEN (1914)

Ernest arranged the picture-taking for that Sunday. They all kept their church-a-meeting best on for the afternoon. Ernest got his father's guns and borrowed two from Uncle George and Pentecost brought three and Voelke one and all the other guys whose fathers had a gun or more succeeded in bringing them along. They had fifteen guns in all to spread around among the twenty-eight guys they rounded up for the picture. They took it on the high school steps, an old official-looking medical diploma passing for the Charter of the Rifle Club.

It was published in the *Tabula,* and Ernest listed McDaniel, Austin and Hussey as "Members in Faculty." Six officers were listed, and the twenty-eight charter members.

There were rumors of some trouble over the hoax, and Ernest had to write a story for the *Trapeze* under the head, BOY'S RIFLE CLUB DISCHARGED. He signed it H.E.

"Leroy Huxham," he wrote, "the newly appointed Secretary of the Boy's Rifle Club, announced that Earle Pashly and Fred Wilcoxen were tied for the lead in the final footing of the season's averages. In the shoot-off held this week Pashly won out and stands at the head of the list. The Boy's Rifle Club is an independent organization com-

121

posed of High School boys and is not in any way connected with the school. The club held its final meeting Monday night and has formally disbanded for the year. H.E."

He used Pashly and Wilcoxen because they had declined to participate. Huxham, he figured, was the guy who was talking it up too much around the school. Well, he got them, he thought, and he wrote "30" under all of it and thought back on the initiation and the picture-taking. Hell, it was the best God damn hoax they'd ever had at Oak Park High. It had been a swell idea. It was more important in the long run than a lot of other things.

# FIFTEEN (1 9 1 4)

That summer, while they were away in Michigan, the war began. It was the subject then discussed at table, in their home, in the village and Chicago and throughout America.

The mahogany dining table was at its full capacity. His mother had brought out the ruby goblets for the water. Oyster soup began the meal, following the prayers his mother offered. She had staged a centerpiece of flowers mounted in a bank of maidenhair ferns. The salad by his father, being as he was the master salad-maker of the family, looked inviting with its mixture of both fruits and vegetables, topped with a crown of shredded carrots and a dressing of his father's own invention made with lemon juice and something that he called his "secret ingredient."

"The Prince of Wales volunteered," his mother said.

America's involvement in the war was a question soon to be decided. His mother was quite proud of Britain's entry in the war. Her forebears had been British all the way on back to the royal Warwick.

"Your mother is referring to the King's eldest son," Dr. Hemingway said. "May I have the ham?"

123

Sunny passed the ham to Ernest; Ernest passed it on. It was made with parsnips, southern style.

"He's in the First Batallion of the Grenadiers," she said.

"Father, what starts a war like this?" Sunny asked.

"I can answer that," Ernest said.

"The question was for your father, Ernest," Mother said. "Would you pass the sweetbreads, please?"

He passed the sweetbreads and his father answered.

"It's a war for which the Germans are responsible," his father said. "It's an outgrowth of prejudice, national prejudice. That may be difficult to understand."

"It was Austria that started it," Ernest said.

"Ernest," said his mother.

"Well, in effect," his father said, "that's right. Austria declared war on Serbia and then aligned with Germany. It's all a most unpleasant business, a failure of man to settle matters in a diplomatic way. But it is my view that all or much of it can be laid at Germany's doorstep."

"I hope we have some more hominy," his sister Carol said.

"Please pass the hominy, Ursula."

"Why is Germany at fault?" his eldest sister asked.

"Do you know what junkers are?" his father said.

She said no and he explained the junkers and the test they wished to bring the German navy to against "an enemy," he said, "just any enemy at all. They want domination, don't you see, wider markets, control of all the seas, the kind of Empire that Great Britain has had. The German Kaiser wants to be the overlord of Europe, don't you see."

"I really don't see why they have to have a war for that," she said.

"I do," Ernest said.

"What was that?" his mother said.

"I understand," he said. "I know all about it." And he did. He had saved the papers, he had read them all from the day the war began.

"I beg your pardon," his mother said, "but are you saying that you are better informed on this matter than your father?"

He said no, not at all, that all he meant was that he understood the way the powers were aligned before the war broke out.

"Let us hear him out, Gracie," his father said. "I think it's good to have the children talk it out and understand."

Ernest swallowed the piece of ham he had been

chewing and he said, "Well, there was Germany and Austria and Italy on one side, and that was called the 'Triple Alliance.' Then there's the 'Triple' something else that includes England, France and Russia."

"Eat your biscuits, Ursula," his mother said.

"But you see Italy was the real question mark," he said.

"Why is that?" Sunny asked.

"Well, Italy didn't like the way that Austria had taken over some of her land. And then the Balkans were a big part of it too."

"Ernest's right," his father said. "The word you couldn't remember, Ernest, was 'Entente,' if I'm not mistaken."

"Yes, that's it," he said. "I couldn't pronounce it right." He laughed a little, looking at his father, and his father smiled down the table at him. Ernest felt proud of all that he remembered of all that he had read.

"This, it seems to me," his mother said, "sounds too much like a history lesson. Here we are with all of this delicious food, and with that simply wonderful salad that your father made, and what we do is talk about the war, which seems to me an unsavory subject for discussion at the dinner table."

"But, Mother, it's the most important thing that's ever happened," Ernest said.

His mother glowered at him. "Now isn't that a slight exaggeration?"

"Well, isn't the war the most important thing that's going on now?"

"Oh, did you say *right now*?" she asked. She was reaching for the honey and she said, "I thought that what you said was that the war was the most important thing that's *ever* happened."

"No, I—"

"Well, I stand corrected," his mother said. "Would anyone be good enough to fetch the cherry jam? I think it might make a nice difference for the biscuits. It's not necessary to stick with honey . . ." She laughed. "I said 'stick with honey,' didn't I? An unintended pun, I assure you."

His sister Sunny laughed. He got up and said, "I'll get the jam." And he went around the table and through the doors into the kitchen. Sure, he'd fetch the jam. Don't talk about the war. No, it's too unsavory. Is it really the most important thing? No, Jesus Christ was. If Jesus was so Almighty God, why didn't he stop the war? Why did he let the Germans cut off the hands of all of those Canadian nurses?

• • •

Later, in his father's office, when he asked his father about the atrocities, the doctor said the stories of the nurses wasn't right. "It was one of those rumors that get started. Mind you, I am not in favor of the Germans marching into Belgium, and I cannot condone many other things they've done. But we have learned that the story of the nurses' hands was started by a nurse who had been captured and who wrote to someone that her hands were sore. That was all there was to it. There was no certainty of any atrocity at all."

"Why don't you like the Germans, Father?"

"It's not the Germans that I do not like. I have heard the atrocity stories, the Belgium children and the nurses and the like, but I am not so certain that they're true. My sympathy is with the other countries of the Triple Entente, since they will be on our side, if we should get into the war. Yet here, just blocks away, are German friends whom I respect and trust as much as anyone. They are devoted to this country that they love, they have a love of liberty not war. The Germans who are junkers and who wish to dominate all Europe—well, it's not the same with them. I have contempt for what they've done and what they hope to do. Someway, even with the power that

128

they have, perhaps because of all the power that they have, they will lose this war. I only hope that we'll not be drawn into it before that happens."

"If President Wilson declares war, can I go?"

"You're much too young, my boy."

"I'm fifteen."

"The war will be over before you're of an age to go."

"But if it isn't, can I go?"

"If it isn't, we'll just have to wait and see. Right now, no one can say."

"Well, I hope I can."

"Well, I hope you'll never have to," said his father.

    •   •   •

But when he read about the war up in his room that night, reading of the killing of the Archduke Francis Ferdinand that was the headline in the paper for the 28th of June, 1914, less than ninety days before, he wanted more than anything to go to war.

# SIXTEEN (1 9 1 5)

That birthday up in Michigan that was his twelfth was the one he would not forget. He would remember it for a long time after. His Grandfather Anson had given him the finest present anyone had ever given him.

Ernest was standing out in back of the cottage. He heard the screen door open and it made a whacking sound in closing. He looked over and he saw Grandfather Anson standing on the porch. He called to him, "Come here, boy." Ernest went over and his grandfather handed him the gun. It was as simple and unceremonial as that. It was the finest present anyone had ever given him. It was the single-barreled 20-gauge shotgun that he would remember as easily as he had forgotten the Henty's *True to the Old Flag* that was given him two years before on his tenth.

Grandfather Anson told him how to use the gun and sat with him to tell him once again about the guns that he himself had used back in the War Between the States. That all seemed a long time back and Ernest would forget some of the stories of the war; but he would not forget the shotgun that he could always touch and take out at night to clean and so he had that much to keep and to remember what he had shot with it whenever he was lonely. That was something he would always have.

• • •

Two years later when the time came that he was lonely and he knew the gun would help he took it out of the closet in his father's office. His father was down in Chicago for the annual meeting of the Surgeon's College. His mother was at the bazaar of the MacDowell Musical Society. Ernest went to his father's office and he took the gun out of the closet and he stood then by the window, raised the shotgun to his shoulder and he sighted a pigeon on the Chambers's house across the street. How do you like it now, Mr. Pigeon, he thought, sighting through the branches of the tree and squeezing slowly on the trigger. But he was thinking in those words that he had thought two years before. Those were the words that he had thought in Union County south of Carbondale.

That was when his father had let him take the gun and shoot the pigeons high up on the rafters of Uncle Frank Hines's barn. If he could prove himself, his father said, with some or all of those —and he did—there were possum yet and coon and there were quail too to shoot, if he could prove himself the shot his father thought he was. And Ernest shot enough to make a pigeon pie. And then his father looked at him with pride, Uncle Frank was there, and took his shells away to keep it all from getting careless and he went away himself to talk with Frank Hines at the house.

Then Ernest sighted on another pigeon and he pulled the trigger on the empty chamber and he broke the hammer spring. Well, Mr. Pigeon, I've really done it now. He picked the pigeons up where they had fallen and he started back on toward the house.

But on the way two farm boys came along. They wore the farmer's kind of overalls, with brass buttons and the pouched and faded knees, and one of them was big and had a thick neck and red hair; the other, and the smaller of the two, stood back a little, guarded: He had a large mole on one cheek. The thick-necked boy asked who had shot the pigeons. He said he had. Then the thick-necked boy took a swing at him without a word of warning. He struck him sharply on the nose. The other just stood back and laughed. Thick-neck walked off then; the other, smaller, mole-cheeked kid skipped on after him, looking back and laughing.

Ernest's nose was bleeding. He wished his gun was loaded. He had kept the gun, they might have taken it. They hadn't got the pigeons either. They had gotten something. He would not forget that day that had gone bad after all the good of it, nor would he fail to remember the thick-necked boy who hit him without warning, and the other mole-faced one that laughed.

• • •

How now, Mr. Pigeon, he was thinking standing now up in his father's office two years away from then and with the shotgun now repaired and with another bird to sight on but not to shoot. He remembered that Uncle Frank had let him fire his A. D. Perry Percussion Sporting rifle with the lettered barrel and the patent-marked frame and proof marks pounded in the metal. He remembered that. The Perry was one of those fine weapons that he would have wanted to own more than anything he ever wanted. Then there was the other gun, the pistol, that still remained protected in the flannel wrapping in the lower drawer of the heavy mahogany cabinet in his father's office.

He put the shotgun back up in his father's closet and he locked the office door from the inside and he went to find the other gun. He knelt down in front of the cabinet and he pulled the drawer open very carefully. There were discarded dulled and broken surgical instruments and Pottawatomi arrow heads, a pack of canceled stamps, there was a snake rattle in one corner of the drawer, and laid on top of everything the old anatomical diploma showing a musculatured man upon a pedestal and on the other side another, skeletal, man, and under them the signature of John Abernathy, M. D. And then there was the gun.

Alongside it was the bullet mold. Grandfather Anson brought the gun and mold back from the Civil War and Ernest's father had promised to show him how to use the mold to make real bullets. But the gun was what he wanted and he weighed it in his hand and thought it must have weighed a pound. A Smith & Wesson .32 that was a forerunner of the Winchester repeating rifle action, his grandfather said, the cartridges being loaded as they were in the later Winchester.

The frame was brass and it had a round side plate and a square butt. The barrel was 3-3/16 inch steel with an octagon body with a rib. It was jointed at the top of the frame and stamped on the rib were the words *Smith and Wesson, Springfield, Mass.* The stock was rosewood or walnut and it wasn't checked, it had a piano finish. Ernest's

father and his father's father in turn had told him
that this gun had been a second-issue weapon that
was carried as a personal pocket pistol in the Civil
War. Ernest's father's father, then, had passed it
on to Dr. Clarence Edmonds Hemingway and
now, when Ernest's father died, he would pass it
on to him. Or it would be passed on to him by his
mother when his father died. Or he would simply
take it.

He would not want his father to die, if that were
possible to avoid by wanting. Only once he had,
and that was in a time of anger. But he would not
want his father's death again nor any time. But
when he had to die, then Ernest would accept it.

He put it away. He wrapped the pistol in the
flannel strip and put it back into the drawer where
he had found it. He was careful not to disturb the
order of the articles that were in the drawer. He
placed the anatomical diploma there on top of
everything as it had been.

The gun would make a wonderful trophy for
his room some day, he thought walking down the
stairs from his father's office.

# SEVENTEEN (1 9 1 5)

Ernest got the telescope from Drexler. It was nothing like grandfather Anson's telescope that was in fact a monocular that dated from the Civil War. Drexler's instrument was newly made and had a rich new look of lustrous brass with fittings that were tooled to perfection. The arrangement was that Ernest, in the trade, would write John Drexler's papers for their English assignments. Drexler was very nervous when he talked about it.

"You can't go making them too good."

"I know," Ernest said.

"Well, we had better go over all of them together."

"Oh, sure."

"I mean we'll have to talk them over so you don't go using no words that I don't understand."

"Keep it simple," Ernest said.

"And they got to be on things I know about when that's what she assigns."

"I know."

"And you won't blow the whistle on it, will you?"

"What kind of a lobcock do you think I am?"

"Okay, but that's important. I mean, I don't want it getting out. If my old man—"

"Right, right," Ernest said.

136

"It's okay then?"

"Absolutely."

"And you agree on what we said?"

"Sure," he said, "why not? Now will you let me have the God damn telescope?"

• • •

If you stood on Lake outside the Scoville Institute you could see quite clearly all the way to Harlem. You could see the picket fence at Schlund's at Lake and Harlem; you could almost count the pickets on the fence. You could see beyond the orchard to the open prairie land. You could use the telescope in shooting. You could also spot with it out at the "skunk hole" lookout and could use it too for spying on the Smyths across on Grove. He could look out the window of his room and look directly over at their corner house. That was what he did the first week that he had the telescope.

He saw the Smyth girl taking off her clothes one night. Betty Smyth, who liked to use the name Elizabeth, was standing at the window in the bedroom on the second floor. He saw much more than he had ever seen before of any girl. It made him quite uneasy. Then when it was over and he felt quite strange about it he lay back in bed and felt his heart beat fiercely in his chest.

Mea culpa. His father had expressed himself upon the subject once and he remembered every word. It made him feel guilty and he was afraid a little, remembering his father's words. His father was the doctor. Well, you couldn't go on with all of that inside of you, with all the girls that stirred you up, and wait until your dreams took all of it away that, after all, you had no way of stopping and no guilt because it was how nature did it. How did celibates control it all their lives? Or did it go away? What a hellish thing if it just all dried up inside you like a pond out on the prairie and you never thought about it anymore. Mea culpa. His father's brother, Uncle Willoughby, had talked about the Chinese eunuchs once, there had been three thousand of them once; but then he stopped the talking when he saw that Ernest was within earshot. Mea maxima culpa. He liked the feeling of the words, the sound of them and then the feeling that they left him with. He said it like a prayer and asked the Lord's forgiveness. Mea maxima culpa.

If that incantation had no meaning, he thought that he was sure to go to hell.

• • •

It was his own possession in a way, he did not want to share it. He did not want to talk about

138

the girl. It was a fragile thing to share with anyone, since they would talk and he would be exposed, and if he talked the whole thing could go
wrong. All the same he watched her on those
nights and felt a little guilty afterwards and never
got the courage up to ask her out. No, he would
never touch it. He wanted it but he would never
touch it. You would have to marry her for that.
You would want some other things to happen but
it wasn't worth the vows that left one bound for
life.

And then he tired of the looking, or tired and
resisted it, and kept his shade pulled down at
night. The window being open, when the wind
blew in the shade it waked him with its flapping
on the sill. And once he saw her and he started
all of it again and felt quite badly of it, thinking
all about it through the morning after. He always
read at night then and he did not use the telescope. He wrote a theme for Drexler that Miss
Dixon graded "A." But in November when he
failed to come up with one assignment Drexler
had to have, John was mad enough to challenge
their agreement.

"You went back on what you said."

"I had my own to do," he said.

"Okay, but you crossed me up, you faker."

"You calling me a faker?"

"Well what you did was what a faker and a cheat would do."

"I hope I got you right, Drexler. I think the faker part of this was your idea, not mine. And if you're saying what I think you are, we're talking about a point of honor and we'll have to have it out."

"You got my telescope, didn't you?"

"You want it back, is that it?"

"Well, you got the telescope and I didn't get my theme like you agreed."

"You got one theme. You got an A on that."

"Yeah, but I'm in trouble on the other one. I'm in real trouble now. I don't know what I'm going to do."

"Well, I'll tell you what *I'm* going to do. I'm going to give you back your God damn telescope. Then I don't want you asking me no favors in the future."

"Don't worry about that."

"I'm going to give it back to you."

"Okay, let's go get it now."

"I let my uncle use it, so we can't."

"Well, let's go see your uncle then and he can give it back to me."

• • •

He had to make it tough on Drexler. That was why he lied. The telescope was in his room. But it was not until the Friday of that week he gave it back to him. And Drexler had to say that he was sorry for the words he used. Ernest glared at him and thought, "There won't be nothing you and I are going to do together, Drexler. You and I are finished."

After that he spread the word that he had written themes for Drexler. Drexler heard about it and he called him names but never to his face. They never spoke again. Ernest felt quite badly of the way it went. He wouldn't have felt so bad except the guilt of it made him uneasy. In giving up the instrument, he felt that he was passing on his own possession, not the object but the thing that he would never talk about. Now Drexler had the instrument and so the thing somehow escaped his private world that somehow was connected with the telescope.

Then perhaps he made too much of it.

Anyway, he felt quite badly of the way it went. But you could not expect to have a friend in everyone. There was a world of friends outside his private world. There were plenty others he had left, and there were others he had yet to meet.

141

## EIGHTEEN (1916)

They took the Avenue Station elevated train No. 1721 down to Chicago. It was six o'clock and no one from the village was around to see them take it. Each had told his parents they were meeting for rehearsals of the Senior Drama Club. They had lied because, although rehearsals had been scheduled, only one of them, Art Thexton, was a member of the Senior Drama Club. Thexton would miss rehearsals on this one. It was his idea that Drama Club rehearsals would provide the best excuse.

"I got to hand it to you, Thex," Al Dungan said.

"I just told my mater," Ernest said with a mock British accent, "that the theatre demanded my presence." He dropped the accent then and said, "So long as my sisters keep their mouth shut, I'm okay."

"Just wait'll you see this 'Sultry Sally' trick," said Savage.

"Yeah, what's she like?" asked Gordon.

"Well, you know that Hope Cavell?"

"*I* don't know her," Dungan said, "but I sure would like to get acquainted."

Everybody knew Hope Cavell, the Classy Jane of the Story Club.

142

"Yeah, well Sally's got just about double every-thing that Hope Cavell has got."

"Yeah?" Gordon said.

"Like the P. T. Barnum Circus girl, you mean?" Art Thexton said. "She had two of everything."

"Like what did she have that there ain't two of what every other moll has got?"

"Heads," Art Thexton said. They all laughed then. They looked around the train. No one else was on it, just the motorman. It was the winter car that they were riding. There were two kinds of "L" trains between Chicago and Oak Park, this one being the closed-up one for winter, and it had two cars, only it wasn't cold enough to have the coalstove going. The summer cars were open and had wooden seats. They were sitting on the cane or rattan-covered seats that sometimes caught your pants if someone cut the rattan; and some kids would come along and do a thing like that. Not them. Not at the chance of getting a report back on their trip when they were saying they were somewhere else. That's why they hadn't brought the lightbulbs: They were known for throwing lightbulbs out the windows down into the street.

"The boy stood in the study hall," Art Thexton was reciting, "he did not hear the bell, and when he reached his English class, the teacher gave him hell."

They all laughed in a raucous, piercing chorus of laughter. Gordon told the story about the girl he met on Dearborn Street down in Chicago. "She said, 'How old did you say you were?' and I told her, 'Well, I just turned twenty-one.' And so she said, 'Well, what took you so long?'" Thexton laughed.

"I don't get it," Dungan said.

"It isn't funny," Ernest said. "McDaniel asked me the other day who gave me the black eye. So I told him nobody *gave* it to me, I had to fight for it."

They laughed and stamped their feet on the floor of the car. The train had gone up on the wooden platform from the street at Laramie Avenue: So now it was in fact the "elevated." They could see the tops of buildings now on either side, and passed close by the ones that had 1895 and other years worked on the big bold sculptured arches that were higher than the tracks.

They were getting into Chicago now and no one else had gotten on. They grew more blatant then and stamped their feet and got a little reckless and obscene of language. They called McDaniel, the high-school principal, dirty names. Thexton had a really scuddy one and Ernest thought of

five or six familiar ones and two that were Ojibwa
Indian curses. Dungan thought of only one. And
they were laughing stridently until the motorman
told them to bring it down. They quieted. But
they were even noisier when they got off at the
turnaround downtown.

They laughed and pulled each other all the way
on down the steps and jostled one another, shouting dirty names, until they reached the place they
had in mind. It was the girlie club on Wabash.
And there was Sultry Sally on the poster boards
in front and then they knew what Savage meant.
Inside the door, the guy who met them must have
been the bouncer. He stood in front of them and
asked what was it.

"Well, we were looking for somebody," Thexton
said.

"Yeah, and who might that be?" the other said.
He looked and talked like a bouncer.

"As a matter of fact," Ernest said, stepping forward, "we were sent in by our Dean, the Dean of
the School we go to, McDaniel's College. We're
supposed to find Jack Pentecost. His mother died
and we're supposed to tell him. He's the nephew, I
think it is, of the owner here. That's what we were
told. We were told to talk to Sally." He turned
to Thexton. "Wasn't that it, Jake? Sally something?"

145

"Sally's the name he gave us, that's all," Thexton said.

"Jack who?" the bouncer said.

"Pentecost," Art Thexton said.

"Well, he ain't here. Anyway, you can't hang around here, this is a private club."

"Yes, sir, we understand," Ernest said.

"We don't want no problems."

"We understand," Art Thexton said.

"But if we could look around, perhaps," said Ernest, "just to see if he was here."

"What's the name again?"

"Pentecost. Jack Pentecost."

"Never heard of him. You say he's Mr. Scarpetti's nephew or something?"

"Might he be here—Mr. Scarpetti?"

"No, he ain't here, that's what I been telling you. Now I'm asking for you punks to get the hell out of here."

"Sir, said Savage, stepping forward to the big man's side, "maybe it would be okay if I just said hello to Sally and asked her. You see, she knows me, she met me once when Jack came in to see his uncle."

The bouncer looked at Savage in a funny way. "You say she knows you?"

"Yeah, oh, sure. I mean she met me once. She

146

knows Jack. She might not just remember me that well, I only met her once, but would it be okay if I just said hello to her again and ask if she's seen Jack? You see, his mother died."

"Yeah, you told me. I ain't never heard of him."

"Well, Sally—"

"Sal's back in her dressing room." The bouncer looked at him. The muscles in his face were moving like knotted strings pulled taut.

"Is she busy?"

"Yeah, she's busy. And you ain't going to see her. On or off."

"Well, maybe Sally knows if Jack's been in."

"Look," the bouncer said, looking beyond them at someone coming in the door, "you punks got no business in this joint. You come in here and I don't know this Jack from nowhere. Now if all you want is to see a little skin, you got the wrong joint, get me, and I don't want no problems out of you."

"We won't cause no problems," Thexton said.

"Now you get back there in that booth back there and you don't make no noise. You keep your mouth shut and you sit back there until she gets her teasing done and then we'll see if what you been telling me is so much crap. And if it is, I'm going to kick your ass out on the street. You got some money?"

147

"Oh, sure, we don't mind paying."

"Well, you ain't going to be sitting back there for nothing," the bouncer said.

•  •  •

They crowded in the dark back booth and watched her strip. The nigger drummer pounded on the snares. The sweat was pouring off his face that glistened in the yellow light. The smoke from those who sat up at the bar and puffed away was drifting up in yellow clouds around the nigger's face. Sultry Sally shook and shimmered and she took it off, she took the pasties off and everything. They were quiet watching her, there always being the chance the law might come in on them, or that the bouncer had it in his mind to turn them in. They were nervous quiet, close and sweating in the dark back booth.

But nothing of the law or bouncer crossing them occurred. And even Sally went along with them, not with their story, since they didn't tell it to her anyway, but with them: She liked young boys, she had one of her own. She let them go with her on backstage, back to her dressing room, and passed around with them a pint of Old Overholt that she had stashed. She called it "Old Overcoat" and it was a hundred proof. She was a swell trick, all right, she had been around some. She liked young boys, her own boy was only eight years old. "You sure look young to have a kid that old," Savage said.

"I take care of myself," she said.

"You sure do," Thexton said.

"You look younger than the molls at school," Ernest told her, taking his turn at the bottle.

"Well, I got a better body than a lot of them," she said.

She was friendly and she liked young boys, so long as you just kept your hands to yourself. "You get to see it, boys, but mustn't touch."

Well, they wished they could have, and they were getting drunk enough to try.

•   •   •

As they left, trying to walk straight right to the door, the bouncer said, "I don't want to see you punks in here no more."

"Yeah," Thexton said back to him when they were outside, "and you know what you can do, you bastard." The door had shut already so the bouncer could not hear what Thexton said.

"Yeah," Al Dungan said, "we hope *your* mother dies."

"If you got one," Ernest said. They laughed.

"Whatever *zoo* they keep her in," Art Thexton said.

149

They laughed and went on down the street. It had cost them plenty, the bouncer taking fifty cents from each of them. It was worth it, though. Hell, the laughs alone were worth it.

They had a swell time on the way back home, as riotous or more than they had had in coming down. And when they got off at the end of the elevated line, Gordon threw up all over the street. "Jesus, Gordon," Thexton said, "the least you could have done was wait until we got up to Mc-Daniel's house. You could have chucked-up on his porch."

"Yeah, why waste it, Gordon?" Savage said.

Gordon said the "L" had made him sick. He smelled terrible. They had to help him home then, taking him behind the house. They got him in the back door and they left.

"He smelled like something rotten," Savage said.

"You don't smell too good yourself," said Ernest.

"That was rotgut rum she gave us," Thexton said.

"It was rye, you dummy," Ernest said.

"Rye or rumgut, it was rotten," Thexton said.

"You're drunk," Ernest said.

"The elevated made me sick."

It was a swell night anyway and it would be worth it even if they all caught hell. That Sally

150

was a real jumpup. They saw everything she had,
or almost everything, and they were close enough
to count the freckles on her bosom. You couldn't
get much closer than her dressing room.

That God damn Savage was good, Ernest
thought; and Thexton too: They were both good.
They could talk about it later. But if anyone ever
went in there and mentioned Pentecost. . .

That thought had them laughing as they broke
up to go their separate ways on home.

It was a long walk home for Ernest and he had
a lot of thinking to do and a lot of fresh air to
inhale. He was lucky to get in through the side
door of the house and up to bed before his stomach started acting up. That was some high-class
rye she gave them, all right. Old Overcoat. He
would never take a drink again, he thought.

The trouble was, you could have swell times like
that but they would never happen quite the same
again.

# NINETEEN (1916)

His mother came into the room and his heart began to race.

"Ernest," she said, "I think we shall have to sit down and have a good talk."

She was dressed for the afternoon's music lesson she would give. It was music-lesson day. It was the Christmas break from school and he would have to stay around the house. He would have to clean the basement and his room. He would have to shovel all the walks. He did not want to clean and shovel and the other things but he would have to do them now because of how things were.

She had come into the dining room. She stood in front of him. He sat on the chair with his back to the window and looked up at her, or at someone who was tall and buxom and whose eyes were china-blue and flecked with something that already made him nervous. He wished that someone else was there, either in his place or hers. Anyone and either place would do.

"I heard about last night."

"What was that, Mother?"

"Don't pretend that you are unawares of what took place last night."

"Well, there was the party at Wilcoxens'. We were celebrating Christmas. Being out of school and all."

"From what I have been taught, and what I have tried to teach my children, Heaven help us, one does not celebrate the birth of Our Lord and Savior Jesus Christ in quite the way you did last night."

"Yes, Mother."

"One does not imbibe of intoxicating wines."

"Yes, Mother."

"Nor does one blaspheme the Lord's holy name and the season of His birth."

He nodded.

"Now," his mother said, "just what exactly was it that you and your undisciplined companions —or perhaps the word is rowdy—what was it that you did to Estelle Fairless?"

He avoided looking up at her. He looked beyond her at the picture on the wall. It was a very fine picture of an English gentleman. "We didn't do anything, Mother." The English gentleman was Charles Hall. He was highly thought of in the family because without him there would not have been an Ernest Hall. "We threw a snowball at her, sure, but she was asking for it. You should have heard what she and her friends called us."

153

"I am not referring to the snowball. I will hear more of what she and her friends called you. But I would like to know what words you and your companions used."

"They were boys' words, Mother."

"Vulgar profanities was what they were."

He looked at her and then beyond her at the picture of the English gentleman without whom there would have been no Ernest Hall. It was not a photograph from life, it was a calotype, that was an early kind of photograph, made of an old engraving or a drawing of the English gent named Charles Hall.

"Profanities?" he said.

"The profanities that were reported to me by two very trusted and reliable sources."

"Well, her mother and her friends are not reliable sources, if you ask me."

"Am I asking you?"

"No, Mother."

"And what exactly did I ask you?"

"Well, Ballinger it was, I think, or was it Golder, one of them had used a word. One of them called her a Jew or something."

"That's not the way I heard it."

"Well, it was a 'damn' Jew, if you want to know."

"Guard your tone of voice, young man. I am not

154

aware that I have given you any reason to become belligerent."

"Mother," he said, looking down at his hands and up at her then, then beyond her at the picture, "I am not being belligerent. And I really don't think you really understand what happened. And whatever happened wasn't any of my fault anyway. I only know that somebody said something to her, that's all. It wasn't anything vulgar or any profanity at all."

"Then can you tell me why she was very ill, too ill in fact to take her supper with her family?"

"Mother, I don't know anything about that. I don't know what happened."

"But you were present when *something* happened."

"That's what I already told you. Ballinger called her a Jew."

"Ballinger? Is he in the habit of calling people Jews?"

"He was trying to be funny, that's all."

"Is there anything else you have to tell me?"

"I can't remember."

She was silent. He could hear her breathing. He had doubled up his hand into a fist. His fingernails pinched the palm of his hand. He knew that she was looking at him.

"Well," she said, "suppose you go to your room until you can remember." Her voice was quite controlled now and she said, "And since you're so popular a figure with the pen around your rowdy social circle, suppose you put down on paper the entire episode for your father and I to read. You can spend the afternoon doing that, and when you've finished your report, I shall read it and decide what must be done."

He went on by her and the picture on the wall and over to the stairs.

He wished sometimes that Charles Hall had never lived.

He took a long time then in getting up the stairs. He counted every step along the way. He halted on the landing on the second floor and looked down at the steps. If he fell down those steps he would break an arm. If he jumped from off the newel post, he might break both arms or legs, but if he broke both arms he wouldn't be able then to write about the trouble-making Jew.

She wasn't a Jew, of course. But Ballinger called everybody a Jew. This year. Last year he called everybody Wops.

He might trace Ballinger's anti-Semitism back to the Romanoffs. He could then branch off into the other bigotries that Ballinger adopted, bring it up to date, and then prognosticate into the future. He could do a glossary on Ballinger's whimseys. He could call it, "Bobby Ballinger's Bigot's Guide to Insults, Methodically Arranged to Entertain the Curious, Instruct the Ignorant, Benefit the Student, Tradesmen and Foreigners who require Barbs for Friends and Enemies Alike."

Or he could do a glossary of Oak Park bigotry against the Papists, Raddies, Atheists, Shonks, and Tipplers, among others. That would take in everyone worth knowing. It would leave out quite a few he knew and lived with. They were in the "Blue Book." He could put the Blue Book under a title like "Dead Souls." The other one would be, "People worth knowing, smoking with, drinking with, and fornicating." But when he sat down at his desk he wrote about his parents' friends in Michigan. He used some dirty words. But they were friends who used such dirty words. He wrote two pages and he read them over, laughing to himself, and tore them out and crunched them in his hands and stuffed them in the pockets of his Mackinaw that was in the closet. Later he would burn them in the alley in the back. Then he wrote a silly verse about that prissy Estelle Fairless. He would tell the others. They would freeze her out.

He began, "Glory to God in the Highest, Peace

on Earth to Men of Good Will. The celebration of the birth of Our Lord and Holy Savior Jesus Christ takes many forms. Sometimes the great spiritual uplift of the Season is defiled by careless and undignified behavior. An example of such reprehensible disregard for the sanctity of the Season would be the Christmas party at the Wilcoxens' Monday night . . . ."

He truly relished writing it and made it long and quite profound. He used all the big words he could find, hoping that a few of them would leave his mother quite confounded. He enjoyed the writing. Besides, it relieved him of the other chores. It was better than having to clean the basement. It was better than having to shovel the walks. But if he had a choice, he would rather be out making trouble with his friends, with Huxham, Ohlsen, Pashly, Ballinger and Wilcoxen. They had something in common: They all hated Estelle Fairless Tattlemouth.

# TWENTY (1915)

The neighbors who were found acceptable that year were asked to come by for a meeting of the families around the Christmas holidays. There were the MacAleers, for one, all the daughters of the MacAleers, meeting with the Hemingways, all the daughters of the Hemingways. There was Lessie, the baby of the Hemingways, and Ernest too, the bad boy of the Hemingways who kept himself up in his room until he saw and recognized the only MacAleer whom he had personally approved.

Her hair was as black and sleek as a crow's wing feathers, long and fine black hair much longer than the village girls' because she came from Michigan and did not know the village ways. Or, if she knew, she did not care. Her eyes were green and he approved. Her skin was white as snow but with faint flushes of a crimson like the bloom of colour on a Chinese porcelain. He approved of Peggy MacAleer and reasonably approved her fine good looks.

Approving then, and while the others were gone on off to tour the house, he introduced himself to Peggy MacAleer. His father was upstairs with Mr.

MacAleer. His mother wanted Mrs. MacAleer to see the rooms and hear about the family, all about the Halls from Edward Hall on down, and some about the Hemingways, from Clarence up to Ernest. Upstairs his father talked to MacAleer about the Hemingways and not about the Halls and showed him the new, now-patented laminectomy forceps that he, the doctor, had invented for the free use of all those surgeons who were serving man in the name of Aesculapius. MacAleer approved. The daughters then were in their rooms with all the other daughters save the one approved by Ernest. He was seeking her approval and was asking would she like to take a walk outside.

He had never liked the basis for approval that his mother had adopted in the pattern of the village that was stolid and, it seemed to him, confined. He thought the questions that were asked before approval were all wrong, that targeted the church, the money, and the clubs. He did not like the gossip that they all accepted as the Gospel truth. He wanted none of that. He did not like the status questions nor the self-appointed juries and the judges of the village. All he liked, and all that he himself approved, was Peggy MacAleer. And she agreed that walking in the snow outside was quite acceptable.

She said she liked Oak Park.

He said it was a big church town.

"I've noticed that," she said, and laughed; and, standing at the street light on the corner, laughing, she was different from the others and he felt quite good to have her all alone like this. He felt she had accepted him.

He said that Oak Park was the same in many ways as were parts of Michigan. Yes, she said, the snow's about the same. He laughed and told her that his family had a summer home in Michigan. He said that she could come up there if she liked and spend the summer with them. He would arrange it. She said she'd like that. He said that would be swell and he would make arrangements to that end.

They talked of football and the school. She liked the school but did not care for football. They talked of writing and she said she liked it. He talked about his writing and he said he planned to be a writer. Oh, she said, that was fine. And she said she planned to be a nun.

A nun? He couldn't believe it. Was she Catholic? Yes, her mother had been married once before; her father, who was dead, had been a Catholic. She was the only one among the MacAleers. He thought that when his mother heard this news there would be a difference in the attitude adopted toward the MacAleers. But not by him.

• • •

And as they walked and talked and he got even then a keen excitement as he listened to her voice not hearing what she said as much as how she said it, he was sure that they were going to get along and know each other for a long long time. That she was Catholic did not matter and he knew that she would not become a nun. He would work it out for them in ways that were unshakable, not like the ways that he had tried and failed. There had been a few, not many, none at all like her, and he would try the ways that others had that did not fail.

The sidewalk on Ontario was covered with an inch of hardened snow. He liked the crunch of it underneath his boots, he liked the sound it made and how it felt. He was feeling very good about the way she laughed and how she laughed at everything he said. He had a good and lively feeling altogether and a keen excitement in his stomach once as she was brushing up against him to avoid slipping on the ice.

Then she made a snowball and she threw it at a tree and then he tried and hit the tree and

162

then she threw a mitten full of snow at him and laughed. He scooped up some snow and gave it back to her. He hadn't meant to really hit her in the face with it. He said that he was sorry. She only laughed and came on back at him and caught him unawares. She had a handful in her mitten and she washed his face with it and laughed. He was surprised that she had turned so playful and he threw some snow at her again and laughed and she rushed back at him and chased him down the walk, around the trees, and tried to wash his face again and that was when he tried to kiss her and they stumbled, holding on together, almost falling, and he only kissed her cheek. She turned away and walked on down the street ahead of him.

"Did I hurt you?" he called after her.

"No," she said and walked ahead. He caught up with her.

"You sure I didn't hurt you?"

"I'm just tired. Can't we go someplace?"

"I hope you really didn't mind."

"I started it," she said.

"I meant trying what I did."

"So it was fun," she said. "Where's someplace we can go?"

He really didn't know why she was acting like that. She was being like the others. They crossed

163

at Lake and Forest and went down to Marion and stopped in front of the Oak Park Restaurant. There was a sign up in the window: "Most sanitary eating place in Oak Park. Ladies invited." Under the sign was another one that said "Closed."

"Well, let's go back," she said.

They went by Sweet's, that was closed, and stopped in front of Cotton's Music Shop and looked in through the window at the instruments. He tried to talk of music and of football and of writing on their way back to the house. She was quiet and indifferent to his monologue. He was disturbed.

"Well, maybe I should just go home," she said.

"I wish there was someplace we could go," he said.

"It's late," she said.

He was quite upset about it and he asked was there anything wrong. No, she said, it was getting late and cold and she had better go on home.

But when he left her at the steps she turned to him and said, "Ernest."

And he went back up to her. She kissed him on the cheek. "Goodnight," she said. She ran on up the steps and opened up the door and went inside without looking back.

•  •  •

164

He walked a long time then and he was even more disturbed, he didn't know what it meant, or why she acted one way then the other. She had accepted him; otherwise, she wouldn't have kissed him on the cheek. He walked the streets then for a long time yet and went around the long block where she lived and crossed the street and looked up to see the lighted window on the second floor and saw her pass in front of it before the light went out.

He was alone and walking in the snow down Kenilworth. The snow was bright and shining crisp and with a clear hard glaze in places where the street lights brightened it. Walking home he thought his loneliness was gone forever now and he was not alone but she was with him. He had been accepted and approved.

•　•　•

But she never went out with him again. He asked her once. She said that she had things to do. He never asked her after that. Later, she went out with Timme. She liked football.

She was a liar about writing. She was a liar about going to Michigan and everything. She liked football. She went out with Timme.

He saw her several times and said hello. She

was cool and indifferent to him. And he never understood. He thought about her many nights and then forgot her. No, he never did forget her. But he tried to think of other things and never liked to hear her name.

After all, he told himself in later months, there were many guys at school who said she was a slut.

# TWENTY ONE (1916)

He sat on the porch and propped his feet up on the railing. Now and again he brought them down to move his body on the swing. The swing would squeak in moving back and forward; that disturbed his reading and he propped his feet up on the railing of the porch. He read of the many books that he had gathered, one in his hand and others on the grey board floor next to the swing. He was going to read as many as he could before the day was over, and read them all, if possible, before the family left to spend the summer up in Michigan. He had a lot to do up there and all of that would make the reading difficult.

She was making it difficult now. The girl who passed the house. It was not enough that she passed at nine o'clock each morning and at five o'clock each afternoon, she had to pass the house at noon, back to where she came from, back to where it was she went.

She had a classic face that bothered him, and dark disturbing eyes. Her nose was straight, as fine and straight a nose as he had ever seen, her mouth was full-lipped, kind of petulant or sensuous. Her hair was reddish-brown, cut straight across the shoulders but with curling at the ends.

167

It flounced as she walked on by the house not looking up at him but walking casually and self-possessed. Sometimes she whistled. And when she passed he looked away at whatever book was in his hand, but there was nothing on the page he looked at whenever she was walking by.

The book he started with that day was Seton-Thompson's *Trail of the Sandhill Stag*. It was the first of that writer that he had been exposed to, but there were others he would want to sample after that. In one week he had read *The Scottish Chiefs, Story of a Bad Boy* and *Sir Toady Lion*. *Sir Toady* was the best, a purely English work for boys and yet a masterpiece. *The Scottish Chiefs* was all too fancy for his taste, a high-falutin style and much lacking in straightforward narrative. But, after all, it was written by a woman. He liked the men author's books, although *Black Beauty* was a good one: then the author was a different kind of woman too.

Many of his early readings of women's works had spoiled him, the ones his mother forced on him, including *Peep of Day*, a pious little tract concerned with God's creation of the world. He was only four or five when that, and *Precept Upon Precept*, were given him to read. He had forgotten them, and all that he remembered from his early

Bible reading were the pictures, one of which, of Jezebel, had stayed with him for many years. The old engraving showed Queen Jezebel falling toward the spears of the soldiery in the street. Her dress was billowing out; above her, at the casements, leered the evil faces of the senseless witnesses.

He had read a lot of Henty and of Kingston and had learned that in boy's stories when the hero faces danger he invariably escapes. Kingston's books enchanted him, one reason of many being that he used the word "three" so often, *Three Midshipmen, Three Commanders, Three Lieutenants,* and the three were almost always English, Scotch and Irish. The Irish boy was almost always quite a jokester, all his jollying expressed in brogue that Ernest liked to imitate. And "three" had been, after all, a lucky number for him up to then.

He liked *The Three Musketeers,* as he and Lew and Samps had taken up their names. *Treasure Island* had been great adventure that he had read late into the night to finish, reading with the flashlight underneath the sheets and blanket, that was the greatest fun he ever had in bed, and he had been exposed to *The Red Eric* in the same clandestine way.

Those were different reading from the Dickens'

works, and different from the Kipling, much of whom he wanted now to read. He had read and memorized the song based on the Boer War ballad of the absent-minded beggar with the words, "Cook's son, duke's son, son of a hundred kings," and he thought the line from Mandalay of "dawn like thunder out of China 'cross the bay" was one of the finest lines ever written by any human being. But he was reading Colonel J. H. Patterson, his second book that day the girl stopped. She was walking by and stopped and said hello to him.

Patterson, D.S.O., whatever those initials meant, was the best writer of East African adventures that he had ever come across. He had been reading everything he could find of and about the Colonel. Patterson had been an engineer who constructed the Uganda Railway in Africa. "Eh, Bwana, simba," Ernest later told the girl. "That means, 'Oh, Master, beware of the lion.'"

They were at her house. How he got there, how it all happened so quickly or at all, he did not know. He had been reading about the lion that carried off the District officer, Mr. Whitehead, and she had stopped to say hello. She had been asking what he was reading every day when she walked by on her way to work, and on her way to lunch and back to work. "You must be in college," she had said. That had pleased him but no, he said, he only liked to read. He talked to her about the reading and it happened then, seeming just as natural as anything, that he was walking with her to her house, she had invited him, to sit with her while she had lunch, to tell her about all the books, to satisfy her great interest in the tales of the Africans.

"Mabarek," he said, telling her of the Swahilis, "is their word for 'blessed one' or one who saves them from the lions."

"Mabarak," she said, pronouncing it as he had.

"Bwana Makubwa," he said. "Great Master."

"Bwana Makubwa," she said. "Bwana Makubwa."

"You had better go on and eat," he said, looking at her sandwich. He drank the sweetened lemonade that she had poured for him and they sat in her kitchen and he told her all about his reading.

"Would you like some milk?" she interrupted, pouring out a glass. He said no and went on talking of his reading; then, when he had finished, she told him all about her work at Cotton's Music Shop on Marion. And all about her life. "We lived in Omaha," she said. "I hated it. It was the dirtiest city I've ever been in. I mean, dirty in every way."

"I've never been there."

"You wouldn't like it. I even feel dirty when I think of it. It's nothing like Oak Park. My father worked for the railroad."

"What work is he doing here?" he asked.

"He isn't," she said, "unless he happens to be here and I don't know about it. We don't know where my father is. There's just my mother and me here, and my aunt, the three of us. He left us several years ago. Mother decided we would come here because of her sister, and because Omaha was so dirty and reminded her of my father and all."

"Who's your mother's sister, maybe I know her?"

"My aunt? Joanna Lublin."

He shook his head.

"She owns this house," she said. "I don't like it. I hope we can get a place of our own. Mother works down in Chicago with Aunt Joanna, for the city, but I decided that I'd rather work out here. I don't mind. The music store's all right. If you like music."

"I hate it," he said.

"Oh, you really hate it?"

"I'm sorry if you like it, but I hate it."

"Well, I'm glad," she said, laughing. "I have no music talent whatever. I am not especially fond of music myself."

172

Well, that was something, he thought, but he was still confused about the way it happened that he was sitting here inside this place with the same girl who had disturbed him walking by the house. He looked at her good mouth and he liked it, and he liked the shaded forbidding look that suggested some strange dark secret in her eyes. It was her age, he thought, she must be nineteen, twenty, maybe twenty-one. He hoped that she would not ask his age.

"Well, let me throw these dishes in the sink," she said, and took her plate and milk glass from the table. "Would you like to see the house?" she said, and waited for no answer, just "Come along," she said, and then he was upstairs with her and she was saying, "I don't have to go back to work if I don't want to. I'll probably get another job, anyway. I'm only making six bucks a week."

"Is this your room?"

"Yes, do you like it?"

"It's very nice," he said.

She turned and looked at him. He felt a little awkward and self-conscious. "I suppose you think I'm forward, compared with other girls you know."

He wasn't sure about her question but he said no, he thought that she was just fine. "There's nothing wrong."

"Well, if you think I'm being forward, you just say so."

"No," he said, "not at all."

"I don't know if you even like being here with me."

"What gave you that idea?"

"I don't know, I guess it's stupid. I suppose you think I'm a forward person or something . . ."

"Not at all," he said.

"Well, maybe you thought I never noticed you before. I did, you know. I noticed you every day I passed your house. I couldn't figure out why you were reading all the time. I thought you were going to college, but then you were always there, and I didn't know why, except I thought that maybe you were crippled up or something and couldn't move off the swing. So my curiosity got the best of me."

He laughed and said, "Well, I'm not crippled up."

"I was hoping that maybe you would say hello yourself someday. Then I knew you wouldn't and that was why I said hello."

"Well, I'm glad you did."

"Are you?"

"Well, sure. You bet I am."

"And are you very glad?"

174

"Sure, I'm very glad. Of course."

"My name's Dorothy," she said.

"Yes, I know . . . Dorothy."

"And you know we're all alone."

He looked at her mouth and a keen excitement stirred inside him.

"Nobody else is here," she said. He nodded and looked around, feeling foolish then. "So you can kiss me," she said. "If you want to."

She clung fast to him as he took her in his arms and kissed her, clinging to him in a way no girl had ever done. She held him long and hungrily and kissed him wet and hard and moved her hips and pushed at him.

He was more at ease after she had withdrawn. He didn't know what to say. He stood there looking at her, less confused now knowing that there was a hunger and a harmony between them now. She smiled at him and he stood there looking at her dark secretive eyes and full wet mouth. He was breathing audibly. He cleared his throat, prepared to speak, but then she said, "You're kind of bashful, aren't you?"

"Well, I guess," he said.

"It's all right. I didn't mean to criticize."

"No," he said.

"It's all right. If you like to kiss me, you can kiss

me anytime you want. Let me tell you something."

He looked at her. "Sure," he said.

"Would you believe it if I told you that you were the very first boy I've kissed since I've been here?"

"Is that right?"

"The very first," she said. "I had a regular boy friend back in Omaha. Robert Lyons. I called him Bobby. But all he ever did was play around. I mean that's all he ever wanted to do. I didn't mind, except I thought we were going to get married. And then when my Dad ran off and everything, and my mother was talking about coming up here, I said to Bobby that if we were going to get married we had better do it then. But he didn't want to at the time. And so I left him."

Ernest sat down on the chair and listened. "It may have been the best thing after all," he said.

"Well, maybe it was. Except I haven't got a boy friend anymore."

He considered that and then he said, "Well, you should have." He was glad to be sitting down. He felt more confident that way, wanting now to be aggressive, feeling right about it.

"That's what I thought," she said. She smiled down at him for what seemed a long time and then she said, "I like you, Ernest."

"Well, I'm glad you do," he said.

"I don't mean you have to be my boy friend. I'm not very smart and not as pretty as a lot of girls."

"Oh, you're pretty. I think you're very pretty."

"Do you?"

"Sure I do. I really do. In fact . . ." He looked up at her.

"In fact what?" she said.

"Well, in fact when you walked by the house a couple times, I thought now there's a pretty girl, all right, a really pretty girl."

"And did you want to meet me?"

"Well, yes, as a matter of fact."

"But it's kind of hard, isn't it? I mean getting acquainted."

"Yes, it is."

"I mean much harder here than in a place like Omaha."

"Well, I guess. I've never been to Omaha."

"You wouldn't like it."

"I guess not."

"It's just an old cow town."

"I don't think I would like it," he said.

"But I'm not Omaha," she said. He looked at her. She was smiling and she moved around the room. He wanted to kiss her again.

"No, you're not Omaha," he said and laughed.

"So maybe you could like me," she said, turning to look at him. "And even if you don't want to be my boy friend, maybe we could get along."

"I'm sure of it," he said.

"Okay," she said. And came directly over to him then. She took his arms and said, "Come here," and urged him to get up, holding at his wrists and then his arms, and then he kissed her and it was the same, but longer, and he got excited. She pulled back and sighed and looked at him. She wasn't smiling and there was something seductive about her eyes and a trembling of her mouth. And then she went on by him to the door and shut the door and said, "Turn your head away."

He looked away from her. How it came about and why he wasn't sure, he was confused, and she kept talking and he had no chance to think, she had him stunned. She said, "There's nothing to worry about, my mother and aunt won't be coming home until five-thirty and we'll be all alone all afternoon."

He felt uneasy and he kept his back to her until she said it was all right, that he could turn around. And when he turned to look at her she was in bed, the bedspread that was lemonish in color pulled up to her neck, and she was smiling at him and she said, "I'll close my eyes while you get ready."

He put his pants and shirt, and then his underclothes and socks, on the cushion of the chair. His heart was beating wildly. Her clothes, her undergarments too, were thrown upon the floor next to the bed: there was no order to it, they were scattered carelessly about. He was uneasy but he knew that he would be all right.

And when he got in bed with her, surprised to find her softness and her warmth, and when they started kissing, he was fine. She was hungry for him and she teased him on with kissing and with touching, she was all right too. The only thought he had was that she had done all this before and many times with Bobby Lyons. That was of no consequence to him, really, except he was concerned that she would find all that he did with her all right, and would say nothing of how awkward he had been.

She said nothing until it had all happened and was over. She sighed and laid her head back on the pillow and she looked over at him on the bed, her mouth quite pouting in its way, quite petulant. She smiled at him then, all she said was, "Mabarak. Bwana Makuba," and she laughed.

• • •

There was a lot that happened after that. Nothing again with her. She and her mother moved away. He was up in Michigan that summer when they moved away. No one would tell him anything about her at the music shop. He went to make inquiry of her aunt. Her aunt Joanna was quite unpleasant when she spoke of her. "Dorothy went back to Omaha," she said. "Her mother didn't approve of it, but Dorothy had a mind of her own."

"Is she getting married or something?"

"I believe she had something like that in mind. I told her mother she was a tramp, but then you know how mothers are. Aren't you the Hemingway boy?"

"Yes, ma'm."

"Well, then you know how mothers are."

"Well, Dorothy said she was going to get some sheet music for me at Cotton's and bring it here. I'm in the school orchestra. She said she'd bring it home and hold it for me here."

"This is not her home," she said. "And she didn't leave anything except a lot of dirty linens for me to clean up after her."

"Well, I guess she just forgot."

"She forgets everything," her aunt said. "She always forgot to clean up after herself."

"Well, thanks anyway. It was sure nice meeting you. I'll say hello to Mother for you."

180

"Don't do that," she said. "Your mother and I are not the best of friends. I know your father, though, and you can tell the doctor Miss Joanna said hello."

•   •   •

He never told him. He never mentioned her. He was relieved to learn that Miss Lublin and his mother didn't get along. He used his father's diagnostic manual one day but that was about as close as he ever got to associating Dorothy and Joanna with his father. "The causative organism," he read in the manual, "is a gram negative diplococcus with its flattened concave surfaces in apposition." That was about as far as he got in that etiology and he never went on to "granuloma inguinal" or "lymphogranuloma venereum."

One day then he noticed, looking in the mirror, his face had taken on some pimples that he hadn't had before. That began to worry him. But then, he thought, everybody, or almost everybody at the school, had pimples at one time or another. Why should he be the exception?

Another day he said to Savage as they walked across Phipp's Field, "Ever know a girl from Omaha?"

"Nope. What of it?"

"Bwana Makubwa," he said.

181

"What the hell is that?"

"It's Swahili," Ernest said.

"Well, what the hell's that got to do with Omaha?"

"You wouldn't understand," he said.

# TWENTY TWO (1916)

The way it was on the school paper, the *Trapeze,* members of the staff changed off as editors. Susan Lowry followed him. In the issue of the 9th he wrote his "Support the Swimming Team" editorial that earned for him a handshake and a thank you from Stew Standish.

He had urged the students to all go on out to New Trier for the meet. He said their rooting would give Standish all he needed to win first place. Stew thanked him on the field later in the day. He had the paper in his hand. "You wrote a swell piece, Ernie," Standish said.

"Well, you're going to win," he said.

"Thanks for the vote of confidence."

"That's all right. You ought to have it from all the others too. But you know how they are."

"I know. Thanks, Ernie," and he tapped him on the shoulder with the paper and started on off trotting to the gate. He was a winner, Standish was. He was one swell guy.

"Hey, Stew," he called after him.

Standish stopped and turned around. "Yeah?"

"Would you do me a favor, Stew?"

"Well, I guess," he called back. "If I can."

"I mean, it's just a favor."

"Sure, what is it?"

"Would you drop the 'Ernie'? Would you call me 'Steen' instead?"

"Well, hell yes, Steen. See you."

He was one swell guy.

"For John's sake," was what he had written for him in the editorial. Standish was smart enough to pick it up.

He wasn't sure the others would get the points he made in what he wrote for Sue on her taking over. He called it, "Ring Lardner, Jr. Discourses on Editorials." He liked the Lardner style and the Lardner humor. Lardner had written some of the funniest stuff ever written in Chicago or anywhere. He was the kind of writer he would like to be. He was better than Howells and Twain; he was surely far superior to Cobb and Riley and the others. Sometimes he couldn't believe that Lardner was only eight miles away down in Chicago. Someday he would meet him.

Someday Ring would drop him a little note to say, "Steen, I am writeing this down at the City Room where half of the boys can't talk english much less read the stuff you been writeing out there and I thot as how you was doing such a smakatowzer job picking up my genius and I don't

mind you understand, I kind of like the flattery,
but laying all jokes to one side I figure as how you
might be comeing by for lunch some pay day.
Your Pal, Ring."

He fantasized about it quite a lot, it was one of
those curious things that kept him in his room
"discoursing" when the others wanted him to go
along with them. He went along with Ring. "Well,
Sue," was what he wrote, getting in with Ring, "as
you are the Editor this week I thot as how I would
write and tell you about how successful I was with
my editorials so you would be cheered up and feel
how great a responsibility you have in swaying
the public opinions.

"You know last week I wrote an editorial on
Support the Swimming Team.

"And in it told about how swell and exciting a
swimming meet was and how thrilling it was and
how the team would appreciate people coming out
and everything like that.

"It seemed like a hot editorial and I thot gee!
there will be a howling mob of rooters at the station for the team and when I came there the platform will be rocked by cheer after cheer.

"So I got a very jazzy speech all ready to say
and it was to start like this. Before I begin,
comma, I would like to explain, comma, that this

185

speech is an oration of the fervid emotional type, comma, so much in vogue, comma, at the time of Henry Ward Wagenknecht, period.

"And I expected at least 500 people and had my speech all ready and do you know how many guys there was there?

"There was one guy and it was Savage and I knew that Savage never read no editorials.

"Well Sue this here is a time of great public danger and everybody had ought to do his part and so I must do my part to preserve this here nation.

"I will write editorials!

"First, I will write one telling all the German soldiers to come over here and we will give them free beer, then the Germans will all right away climb up on the top of the alps so as to get as far from here as possible and then I will read them another editorial telling them to hold on tight and they will all be all let go and drop into the Rhine and be drowned and their dead bodies will be washed down into the Helespont.

"And in this way our country would be saved and it would show the power of the press. Is that not a good idea do you not think?

"Well, Sue, I had better close now on account that I want to get a guy in free to the class Play

and so I will write an Editorial saying that nobody
be admitted for less than five dollars.

Yours Sin Searedly

Ernie Hemingway.

"P.S. Please note that in this letter I have not
referred to no guys but Savage and this is not because I ain't ascairt of Savage. But I do not think
he will get sore because he is a friend of mine and
sits by me in Commercialized Law. E.H."

• • •

Later he was sorry he had written it. Nobody
told him it was funny. No one came up to him like
Standish and tapped him on the shoulder with the
paper and said "Swell job, Steen," or anything.
Well, he would not bring it up. That was the way
with writing. He guessed it was the way with everything. In a year's time Standish too would be forgotten for all his glories on the swimming team.
In a week, what he had written would be all forgotten. Only Wagenknecht would remember.

"Henry Ward Wagenknecht" was what he had
called Edward Wagenknecht, on account of how
stuffy he was, and because Eddie figured he was
going to be a writer too. Edward passed him in
the hall one day and gave him a dirty look. That
meant he had read the editorial. Wagenknecht was
smart. He wasn't supposed to like it. He got the

point. No one else did but Henry Ward Wagenknecht was smart. He was smart enough too not
to say anything. He knew better than to start a
fight with Hemingstein.

Well, Ernest was sorry that he wrote it and when
Eddie passed him in the hall that day he felt uneasy when he thought of it. It was a spiteful and
a petty thing to do. He did not want to be that
way. Eddie was smart. Eddie ignored him. Eddie
would be the writer; and he, Hemingstein, would
be sitting there expecting Ring Lardner to drop
a card inviting him to dinner. Only it wouldn't
happen. The thought of it, however much a fantasy it was, kept him writing like the Ringer. You
had to hold onto the fantasy because the writing
was ignored and left you. But the fantasy remained. There was nothing wrong with that. It
made more writing if you used it. It was something that you had to have. As for the writing,
he could always do a better job, or try, and hope
that someone would come up to him and say that
it had made them laugh.

He sat down at his desk and wrote a note to
Wagenknecht. He never gave it to him. They were
rivals. Never give your competition no edge, he
thought tearing up the note. That's the way Stew
Standish would have put it.

188

## TWENTY THREE (1 9 1 7)

In the morning was the rain, and it was the rain that saddened him, and the rain was like Rebecca's tears. It was the sadness that had come to him the night before. The sadness was the same with him, and thinking of her brought it back. His mind went crazy with the sadness and the rain. The rain it was that made him think of her; the thinking made him crazy-sad. And the rain it was that made him think. And the rain was like her tears. And he had made her tears. And now the rain was making them.

She was a girl his sister knew. Rebecca Cunningham. She was over at the house that night, the night they had the party for his eldest sister Marcelline who had enrolled in Oberlin and would be going there in the fall. It was the Oberlin acceptance party they were giving and he hoped to get the hell away from it. The party did not interest him. It was the kind he was avoiding now, rejecting every thing he used to do, rejecting every one he used to like, rejecting every place he used to go. Rejection was the posture he adopted and continued to show, indifference and aloofness, coldness too. And cruelty. And on this night he thought that he would play it all the way.

189

His sister caught up with him at the door as he was leaving. "Ernie, wouldn't you like to meet my friends?"

"No thanks."

"Come on, Ernie, let me introduce you around."

"No, Sis. I don't want to meet them."

"Come on, it's a party, Ernie. There won't be many more. If any. And the girls would like to meet you."

"I've already met them."

"No, you haven't. There are two girls from Oberlin. I know you haven't met them. I told them all about you."

"Sure, well that's another reason I don't want to meet them. I don't want you telling anyone about me. All I want is to be left alone."

"All right, then *be* a stick." And off she went. She turned away from him and walked on off and she was plenty mad.

He liked the feeling that it gave him.

• • •

But on his way back home, after he had walked what seemed a thousand blocks, and thought about the hundred books that he had read that year, and all the times both good and bad that he had known at school, the bad times more than good, in number and in what he thought, he ran

190

into Rebecca Cunningham. She was walking home. He ran into her at the corner north of the house, under the street light on the corner.

"Aren't you Marce's brother?"

Well he stopped and said, "That's right."

"I'd hoped to meet you at the party. My name's Becky Cunningham."

"I see," he said. "Where you going?"

"Home," she said. "I live in River Forest."

"You walking all the way?"

"It isn't far. I don't think we ever met. I'm at Oberlin, where Marce's going. We might be roommates. I'm sure she'll like the school. I think it's perfect for her talents."

"Talents? What talents does she have?"

Rebecca laughed. "She said that you were funny."

"I'm not funny."

She looked at him quite carefully and said, "Well, she has many talents, you know that."

"No I didn't," he said. "You see, we don't really like each other."

"Well, she likes you, I know *that*."

"No she doesn't. It's all pretense. She really hates me. She tried to kill me once."

Her laugh this time was tentative, almost a gasp.

"I'm telling you she tried to kill me."

191

"I don't believe it," she said. "How could she have possibly tried to do a thing like that?"

"She baked an apple pie for me," he said.

She laughed then, with relief and overmuch. He laughed too. Well, hell, he thought, the pose just wasn't going to work with her, there was no point to it. Not with her there wasn't. She would laugh at what he said.

•  •  •

"Look," he said, "I'll walk you home."

She laughed at everything he said. They had a long walk and they did a lot of talking; he did most of it. He told her all about the troubles he had gotten into at the school. "And then that night at Savages'," he told her, laughing, "we were going to paint this wall down in his basement, see. To make a den out of this one big room. The rest of it was painted. So Savage got five of us guys together. We had two bottles of wine he snuck out of his old man's cellar and we were getting drunk and everything and so instead of painting the wall we started to paint prehistoric people on it, Neanderthals and everything. I did this ape man with the big club and Savage did the ape's wife and she was the ugliest critter you ever saw. Savage said it was modelled after his mother." He laughed

192

as he recounted it. She laughed along with him
and seemed to have accepted him absolutely.

"Well, this is it," she said. "That's our place
there."

"Gee, that's a nice house. You must be rich."

"Well," she said, "I guess we won't be seeing
each other again. Unless you get up to Oberlin to
visit with your sister."

"It doesn't make any difference." He didn't even
know why he said it.

"Why do you say that?"

"I just meant it doesn't matter. I won't be visit-
ing her or anyone else."

"Well, I'm sorry," she said. "Is there some special reason?"

"Plenty," he said. "I'm not especially fond of
Maaz. As a matter of fact, I don't like any of my
sisters."

"Now you're joking. You can't mean that."

"I mean it," he said. "I hate my mother too."

"I don't believe it."

"You don't believe anything, do you?"

"What?"

"You don't believe anything I told you. You let
me walk you home because you wanted to show
off your big rich house and your big college education and everything. Maybe you thought I'd

want to kiss you and you could turn me down. That would have made you happy, wouldn't it? Well, I didn't want to kiss you and I never would. I didn't even want to walk you home."

She was already crying by the time he finished. She looked at him, her eyes were moist, she said, "You're the rudest person I've ever met."

And when she reached the porch, running all the way on up the steps and all along the walk and quickly up the other steps that went up to the porch, he could hear her crying even then from where he stood.

•  •  •

That night he wondered why he had done it. His mind was all confused. It gave him trouble and he couldn't sleep. He would find her and apologize. But then he got to sleep and when he wakened it was raining. He was afraid to see his sister. He lay in bed. He was afraid to get up from bed and go downstairs. He wished his sister would go on off to Oberlin and he would never see her. His mind was still confused. He could not accept what he remembered of the night before. Insanity, he thought. It was insanity. His mother got that way sometimes. He was confused.

It was the rain that saddened him. It fell in torrents on the roof. He could hear it, being as his

194

room was at the topmost point, the angled roof above his room resounding with a noise like muffled drums. The rain was like her tears. The sadness was the same with him, the sadness he had known the night before. And thinking of her brought it back.

He got up from the bed and sat down at the desk. He listened to the rhythm of the rain and then began to write. "Rebecca, when I think of what I've done, I ask myself, 'Is she the last of all the people that you ever want to meet?' I answer, 'Yes, because I am not worthy of her friendship or respect.' Forgive me. I ask myself, 'Is she one of the most gentle and deserving people you have ever met?' I answer, 'Yes, because she tries to understand my strangeness.' Forgive me. I ask myself, 'Is she among the most beautiful and lovely creatures in the world?' I answer, 'Yes, because she has never been exposed to ugliness like mine before.' Forgive me."

He never signed the letter. It was part of his confusion. Never gave it to her. Never saw the girl again. Never knew what happened with his sister and the girl.

● ● ●

But as the morning gathered darkness with the clouds, his mind began to function in a way that he

195

had never known before, and then he kept on writing and his mind was less confused, and wrote a story that began with rain.

And writing it he heard the muffled rhythm of the rain upon the roof and then he listened to the voices of the people he had known, their voices and some laughter, and there was a meaning to the laughter that he suddenly discovered, a meaning and a beauty to their lives that he had never known before, and listened, hearing knowing them and, for the first time, writing them: writing then as he had never written, he felt a stirring of a kind inside him, of a kind he'd never known before. Not in the way he knew it now. There was a clarity; a sharpness; thought and spirit merged. And all the strength inside him grew and focussed on the subject he was writing on; then a kind of exaltation hovered over it. The something growing stronger, all the brightness coming into focus, all exalting.

He had the answer. Others told him once. That meant nothing now. Now he told himself. He knew.

He knew that if he could do what he had done, write of the voices and the laughter, the flood of life, life exaltant, then he had the answer, nothing in the world could stop him, if he could move it fast enough, himself move fast enough, and push some other ways.

The morning gathered darkness with the clouds.

The rain fell in a rhythm on the roof.

Rebecca writhed.

# TWENTY FOUR (1917)

The sky was low and it was going to rain. It was a dismal morning, he could see the clouds were moving in. He saw them from the window of his third-floor room. The sky was darkening, the clouds were moving in and moving slowly to the west. He could see his sister on the street below. Standing at the window of his room upstairs he saw his sister crossing over Iowa Street to Grove and on her way to Lake. She had a pack of belted books all bound securely with the leather belt that he had given her. They were books that both of them had borrowed during school. She was returning them to Scoville and he saw her go beyond the corner house and then himself got dressed to go on down the stairs and out to do the things that he would have to do now that school was out. School was out for summer and for good, for him and for his eldest sister, Marcelline.

He walked along the elm-lined walks from Kenilworth and Iowa Street and on past Oak Park Avenue and straight on, crossing Euclid then, then Linden and to East. He turned on East to go on over to the school. It was seven blocks, or close to eight from home.

He would have to gather up the things that he had left inside his locker in the basement of the school. He took the route past Euclid then, and on the other streets, because the other way was how he went the day before and everything was different now. He had come to his decision and he knew the way to go. The way he took in walking to the school was not the same because he did not want to see the people and the places he had seen the day before. He wanted everything to change, including that. Now that school was out. Commencement week had ended. The other things had ended too. The old alliances were gone, and now he knew that he would go his way alone.

His father had some plans to drive the Ford to Michigan. He wasn't sure that he would go along with them although it meant confronting them and their support was what he had to have if he was going to carry out his plans. The summer up in Michigan was something that he had, and even wanted probably, to do, because it was the final time if he was going to go his way alone.

Well, however you might look at it, it was a new beginning and he had direction and a destination now. He did not want those future glories that his father had worked out for him, not Med school nor the other schools that others of his class were headed for. He had decided for himself. There had been suggestions but it was he who had decided in the final resolution and he hoped there were no further indecisions and revisions from their self-appointed planning board.

He walked on down past Euclid and past Thexton's house and thought about the times they had, the times they ran away that had the forest rangers after them and when they went into Chicago and old Gordon was the only one got punishment for being drunk. He walked past Linden and he thought about Phil White. He knew that bitterness could pass but he expected fully that it might come up again and stay with him a long time yet. He went on by the MacAleers' new house, there were heavy elms surrounding it, regretting all of that with her that might have been so different. Then his mother would have made a big thing out of it and cut him up again with all the emphasis on dignity distilled from all the holy Halls: the never-ending lies about the lineage that made you think yourself apart from all the rest. He had learned already that you were the better or the best because of what you had inside of you and no one that you came from made you any bigger in your class or any higher on the scale than any of the others who had come from other lines. He

spat against a tree and went on by the house
where Estelle Fairless used to live before they
moved to New York state and he remembered
what they did to her and now he was remorseful
over it because her spine was shattered from the
swimming accident out on the lake out by the
Indiana Dunes. Then he thought of the others
who had been unlucky. He hated that, remembering the worst of all that happened to the better
ones, or ones who hadn't been so bad compared
to some. He turned on East to go on over to the
school and thought of Voelke, what a lump, who
had been truly swell compared; and Willards too,
old Dorothy did so many decent things for him,
and Swanson and Merservy and Al Speelman.
Well they were going to have to face it now as he
was facing it and all the lucky ones were going
to Amherst, Dartmouth, and to Yale, places he
had never seen but thought of them as very east-
ern and all far enough away.

From home. Well that was it, you had to leave
it even if in leaving you would miss the good ones
and the good times too. You had the memories to
carry with you and you could always sift through
them in time and keep the better ones alive. The
hunting and fishing and the hiking and the family
liking what you did; the sharing up in Michigan

and, less often, here; the sharing anyway and helping them, his sisters; and the teaching of his little brother and the others none of whom were family but every bit your own, like Proc and Lew and Thex. He walked much faster trying not to think about the good ones now because they seemed to be much better now that he was leaving, and in leaving then, he thought, he would not want to tell them, not until he had his ticket on the train. You couldn't tell them yet unless you had a story that would make it sound much different than it was and he was lacking that.

He was lacking plenty now that he had known, and even what had happened seemed less real of those other days and nights. He thought of many of them as he walked, of good and bad, thinking fondly of the good, his own, the people and the places that he loved, and something of his hates, his minor triumphs and his escapades. He had a lot to take with him, he thought going on then on up the steps into the school.

●   ●   ●

Going out then a little after, walking down the steps a final time, he had a lot to leave, he thought, and walked on up to Linden, looking back a final time, and walked on north to turn up at Superior and go on north on Euclid to Augusta under vaults of full-leafed trees that sheltered him against the starting rain. It fell upon the brick-paved street that glistened from the wetness and it spattered on the walk and leaves and he began to run to keep from getting wet.

Running with the leather satchel Maaz had given him and shifting it from one hand to the other, it banging at his legs; he slung it up across his shoulder and he felt its weight against his back, the satchel heavy with the cleated football shoes that never had been big enough for him, and track and tennis shoes, the boxing shorts and wrappings for his hands and books that he would pass on to his little brother hoping he would learn from them the way that he had not.

In the satchel was the yearbook too, the *Tabula,* that he would soon surrender to his mother with his "Prophecy" that she would never fully understand. So she could read the caption to her friends that Sue had written for his picture.

"But then he never learned to play the cello," she would say.

"That's right," his father would affirm.

He wished that Sue had called him Steen: "None are to be found more clever than Steen."

If she had written Steen he would have kept the *Tabula.*

"You see," his mother possibly would say, showing it to all her friends, "my daugher Marcelline wrote this fine essay on the Chinese . . . ."

But he, who never learned to play the cello well, had written only six confounding pages to his sister's brilliant four.

Sure he was Class Prophet, only there wasn't much that he had prophesied would come out right, not for yesterday nor profit for tomorrow. He didn't know a fragment of the truth about tomorrow. Nor today, nor yesterday either, or what he had to leave, or why, or how and where it went, or why, or anything.

He hurried on into the house and everything was wet except the contents in the leather satchel Maaz had given him. His clothes were wet, his head was wet, and water dripped on off his pants on down into his shoes.

Except he knew that he was going to go to Kansas City.

If he knew that much, he knew enough. If he knew that much he knew as much as God and more than all the other Hemingways. Well he had to tell them. There wasn't any getting there without the telling them.